She'd clouded his thoughts until he'd finally decided he had to do something about it. He was now determined to convince her that they needed to spend time together and figure out what was between them.

Daniel placed his wineglass on the cocktail table in front of him and reached for one of Angela's hands. "Don't deny yourself, deny us, because you're scared. I know we're in uncharted territory here, but there's something between us. You must feel it like I do."

He watched her bring her wineglass to her mouth for a sip and realized her hand was shaking. Daniel wished he were that glass. Wished he could take her lips with his and suck the sweet juices off them. But he didn't want to come on too strong or she would pull away.

He released her hand and rose to his feet. "Think about it."

"You've certainly given me a lot to consider," she finally said.

"I know, but when I feel strongly about something, I go after it."

"And you want me?"

Those beautiful brown eyes of hers looked up at him expectantly.

Dear Reader,

Miami After Hours is the first book in the dynamic new Millionaire Moguls series featuring three heroes: Daniel Cobb, Joshua Delong and Ashton Rollins. In *Miami After Hours*, you'll meet sexy millionaire Daniel Cobb. Daniel has been hurt in the past by unrequited love, but I infused him with just enough heart that he's willing to risk an affair with our feisty heroine and his mentee, Angela Trainor. The chemistry between the pair is off the charts. Hope you enjoy all those steamy love scenes!

I've threaded a great subplot involving who will run the Miami Millionaire Moguls organization into the book. If you want to know how it will play out, you'll need to read the next two installments in the series: *A Miami Affair*, Joshua's story, and *Secret Miami Nights*, Ashton's book.

Visit my website at www.yahrahstjohn.com to download my latest ebooks or write me at yahrah@yahrahstjohn.com for more info.

Enjoy,

Yahrah St. John

Miami After Hours

Yahrah St. John

H HARLEQUIN® KIMANI™ ROMANCE

Recycling programs
for this product may
not exist in your area.

ISBN-13: 978-0-373-86502-4

Miami After Hours

Copyright © 2017 by Harlequin Books S.A.

Special thanks and acknowledgment are given to Yahrah Yisrael
for her contribution to The Millionaire Moguls miniseries.

HARLEQUIN®
™ www.Harlequin.com

Printed in U.S.A.

Yahrah St. John is author of twenty-two books. St. John is the recipient of the 2013 RT Reviewer's Choice Award for Best Kimani Romance for her title *A Chance with You*. When she's not at home crafting one of her sexy romances, she can be found in the kitchen cooking one of her gourmet meals discovered on the Food Network for her fiancé. Or, this thrill junkie can be found traveling the globe seeking out her next adventure.

A graduate of Hyde Park Career Academy, she earned a bachelor of arts degree in English from Northwestern University. St. John is a member of Romance Writers of America, but is an avid reader of all genres. She lives in sunny Orlando, the City Beautiful, where there's great weather all year round. For more information, please visit www.yahrahstjohn.com.

Books by Yahrah St. John

Harlequin Kimani Romance

Two to Tango
Need You Now
Lost Without You
Formula for Passion
Delicious Destiny
A Chance with You
Heat Wave of Desire
Cappuccino Kisses
Taming Her Tycoon
Miami After Hours

Visit the Author Profile page
at Harlequin.com for more titles.

To my bestie and sister, Dimitra Astwood,
for being strong in your darkest hour.

Chapter 1

Daniel Cobb strode through the glass doors of Cobb Luxury Real Estate, confident and poised in a custom Tom James suit and Ferragamo loafers. He'd started the company with the commissions he'd made while working with his father. Now he was the proud owner of his own thriving and highly sought-after real estate company.

Daniel only accepted wealthy clients looking for the most high-priced condominiums and homes in Miami. Anyone walking through the double glass doors of his agency knew what to expect. A skilled agent with expertise in the marketplace. As head broker, he'd hired only six other agents because he wanted to ensure that his clients received the most discriminating customer service.

Determined to make Cobb Luxury Real Estate the premier firm in Miami for luxury homes, he was at the office early in the morning and late into the night, reviewing numbers and overseeing staff. Along with his commitment to Prescott George, a men's club he belonged to, that left very little time for play...or for women. Not that he was celibate. He had the odd date or two, which usually ended up with a beautiful female in his bed and a smile on his face. But he had no time for serious relationships.

He'd made sure of that after he'd foolishly fallen for Mia Landers back in college. She'd been petite and adorable, with dark doe eyes and a shy demeanor. Daniel had been instinctively protective of her, but Mia had been head over heels for Ashton Rollins, a fellow student of Daniel's who paid her no attention. Daniel had thought if he bided his time, Mia would see the light. She hadn't and had died in a tragic car accident later that year, leaving Daniel alone with his anger and regrets. And his guilt. If he'd managed to keep Mia away from Ashton, would she still be alive? Daniel would always wonder if he could have done more.

After that tragedy, he'd focused all his energy into building an empire. He wanted to own homes around the globe, and that required lots of money, especially if he wanted to travel.

Thanks to the phenomenal last few years, he'd added a penthouse in Key Biscayne to his portfolio. The building housed only three other units and was surrounded by nothing but glass. It was sleek, modern and sophisticated. Just like him.

"Good morning, Myrna," he greeted the receptionist as he passed by.

"Good morning, Mr. Cobb." Myrna smiled back at him as he made his way to his all-glass office facing downtown Miami.

Myrna was easy on the eyes, which was exactly what

Daniel wanted to portray to prospective clients. However, he wasn't fooled by the cool blue eyes, slick blond hair and slender figure. At twenty-five years old, Myrna was not only smart and capable, she was hungry for more. He could easily see her obtaining her Florida real estate license and becoming one of his agents. He recognized the drive; he had it himself.

Closing his office door behind him, Daniel walked over to the window and looked out over the bay. He'd always been driven to succeed, but it hadn't been easy. Even though it appeared as if he came from rich parents, he'd been raised in a middle-class family. And once his parents had divorced, because of his father's philandering ways, he'd been shuffled between two middle-income households.

Daniel grew up learning the business from his father, Kenneth Cobb, who had a small real estate company in Fort Lauderdale. He'd been required to man the phones during school breaks. If he hadn't, he wouldn't have gotten a chance to spend any time with his father, who, when he wasn't working, was more concerned with the ladies than his only son.

Once he'd graduated from Nilson University with a degree in finance, he'd decided to open his own firm, except *he* would cater to a select niche of young, hip and most of all wealthy buyers and sellers. Cobb Luxury Real Estate was a frequent poster on Facebook, Instagram and Twitter. And thanks to meeting the illustrious Rollins family, a connection he'd made in college, the doors to the rich and famous had been opened to him. Too bad that connection had cost him the only woman he'd ever loved.

"Mr. Cobb," his assistant, Mary's voice echoed from

his phone's intercom. "The Archers are here to meet with you."

"Tell them I'll be with them in a moment." Daniel stood up, straightening his tie and smoothing his designer suit even though nary a wrinkle could be found on it.

The Archers were new clients who had been referred to him by the Grants, a couple to whom he'd recently sold an amazing five-thousand-square-foot condo. He was grateful for the referral because the Archers' price range was six to nine million dollars, which would mean a substantial commission for him.

Daniel swung open the doors and got started doing what he did best. Conquering the market.

Real estate agent Angela Trainor rolled her eyes as she watched her potential buyers, the Harrisons, nitpick the modern kitchen of an exclusive penthouse in Bal Harbour. Did they even know what a find this was? Homes like this rarely came on the market, and the fact that she'd found this for them should have been a feather in her cap. Instead they were finding anything that they could wrong with the luxurious condo.

"Do you see the handles on these kitchen cabinets?" Mrs. Harrison turned to her, and Angela immediately resumed her sales persona. "They're ghastly."

"Hardware is easily changeable to suit whatever design concept you desire," Angela responded.

Mrs. Harrison shook her long straight black hair that hung down her back and fiddled with the diamond-studded bracelet on her thin wrist. The bracelet had to cost more than Angela made in a year! And that wasn't the only expensive bauble she wore. The woman was draped in jewels, no doubt by her wealthy husband who appeared to be about thirty years her senior.

"I don't know about this, darling," Mrs. Harrison said, turning to her husband. "You know I want something move-in ready."

"Move-in ready?" Mr. Harrison chuckled. "Julia, you know as soon as we purchase, you'll be gung ho to have the entire space redesigned. I'm with Angela on this one. Surely the hardware is a little nuisance we can easily overcome?"

Angela moved in for the kill. "As you know, this neighborhood is considered the crème de la crème by *Miami magazine.*" She knew Mrs. Harrison was one of those women who cared about social standing among her peers. "And with the amenities like the twenty-four-hour concierge, gourmet market and state-of-the-art fitness center, you won't find a place quite like this. Come, look at the view," she said, motioning the couple toward the terrace so they could once again admire the panorama of Miami Beach.

"Give us a few minutes, Angela," Mr. Harrison said.

Angela nodded and quietly left the terrace to give the couple privacy. With any luck, they'd agree to purchase the penthouse. Her stomach was in knots just thinking about the fifty-thousand-dollar commission that awaited her if the couple accepted the asking price.

She'd never sold a property as expensive as this one. With her earnings from this commission, she would be close enough to the amount she needed to buy her own luxury condo in a new building in Brickell near downtown. Meanwhile she was living modestly in a one-bedroom apartment in Coconut Grove.

The Brickell developer was known for its luxury appointments including gourmet kitchens and sumptuous master baths. Angela couldn't wait to be the proud owner of one of the condos, which was what had prompted her move to Cobb. She'd known that selling $500,000 homes to middle-class clientele at the larger real estate firm where she'd worked for nearly three years wasn't going to get her there. She needed the big commissions that she pulled down with Cobb Luxury Real Estate, and now she was finally moving in the right direction.

Of course she had to dress the part and had to upgrade her wardrobe to ensure that Daniel Cobb would take notice and consider her a good fit for his firm. He'd personally handpicked every agent who sold for him, and Angela had considered herself lucky when he'd agreed to hire her. He'd told her she needed some grooming and had vowed to take her under his wing. In the interim, Angela was trying her best to fit in.

Everyone in the office wore designer clothes, and Angela could be no different. She'd taken a portion from her savings and gotten a complete makeover. Her usual brown hair had been stylishly cut by a top hairstylist in Miami and highlighted with honey-blond streaks. She'd gotten a makeup lesson from an artist who worked on the rich and famous, and now Angela knew how to artfully do her makeup to make it appear as if she were barely wearing any.

Changing her clothes was easy, because Angela always had a love for fashion. She'd just had to raise the bar. And she had. She'd raided several designer boutiques until she now had a stylish array of suits, dresses, skirts and tops that bespoke her new role as a luxury real estate agent.

Today, to impress Mrs. Harrison, who would recognize a designer outfit a hundred feet away, Angela was wearing the latest Marc Jacobs dress along with a pair of Gucci sandals that had come on the market a month ago. The entire outfit had cost Angela a substantial chunk, but it would be worth it if she made this deal.

Suddenly the doors to the terrace slid open and the Harrisons walked in.

"Have you made a decision?"

"We'll take it," Mr. Harrison replied.

And just like that, all of Angela's dreams for her future started to come true.

Daniel watched Angela Trainor drift past his line of vision. New to his office, she was under his tutelage and coming along rather nicely. He'd handed a plum client like the Harrisons over to her with faith that she could seal the deal. He hoped he hadn't missed the mark.

Angela knocked on his door even though it was open and poked her head inside. "Are you busy? If so, I can come back another time."

"No, c'mon in." He motioned her forward.

As she approached, Daniel couldn't help but admit she was a fine-looking woman, but then again he only hired the best. He had an image to protect. That's not to say that he couldn't appreciate a thing of beauty from a distance. And he certainly appreciated Angela.

She wore an elegant sheath that hugged all her curves, and her shoes were high enough to do wonders for her long, toned legs. Then there were her smooth tawny-colored skin, honey-blond hair that looked like it had been kissed by the sun and those lips that had Daniel thinking thoughts he shouldn't.

He blinked rapidly, refocusing. "So? How'd it go?"

A large grin spread across her full lips, showing even

white teeth. "Slam dunk," she replied. "The Harrisons want to make an offer on the penthouse. I'm putting together a comparative market analysis so we can negotiate the price."

"Excellent," Daniel said. "I knew I made the right decision in hiring you."

To some, he'd taken a risk. On paper, Angela Trainor was relatively green. With only one year of college and a varied work history, Angela might appear flighty to some. But since obtaining her Florida real estate associate's license a few years ago, it seemed as though she'd found her calling. She was just the breath of fresh air he needed to ensure the firm stayed relevant.

"Was there ever any doubt?" she asked boldly.

He liked her confidence and tenacity. She would need it in this business. "Don't get too cocky. This is only your third high-value sale."

"But it won't be my last."

"Ambition is good," Daniel returned. "You'll need it because this business can be rather cutthroat, dog-eat-dog, if you know what I mean."

"I do. This isn't my first rodeo, Daniel," Angela responded. "Working at one of the largest firms in the country taught me that I'll have to make my own luck."

"Good to hear," Daniel said. "Now you just have to seal the deal and get to closing." He knew that just because an offer had been made didn't mean the sale was a foregone conclusion. Deals could fall apart before closing. Not that it ever happened to him. Daniel took every precaution to ensure that it didn't.

"Of course."

"Speaking of deals, I've recently signed a new client,

a developer that has tasked me with selling out the eighty condos in his building in downtown Miami."

Angela's eyes grew large. "Sounds amazing."

"It is, but it's a challenge. The lower-end condos go for a thousand a square foot, and the penthouse is fifteen hundred a square foot."

"Well, if anyone can do it, you can."

Daniel appreciated her ego boost. "Thank you, but praise is not the reason I'm mentioning it."

"No?" She quirked a brow and he couldn't resist returning with a grin.

"I want you to work on the project with me."

"You do?" Astonishment was evident in her voice.

"Why do you think I plucked you away from that other firm? It was to give you the opportunity to grow and to learn under my tutelage."

"I'm ready for whatever you want to offer me." She blushed as soon as she said the words, no doubt because he could certainly take it to mean something other than work. Something like what he could offer her in the bedroom.

Where had that thought come from?

It was his cardinal rule to never date any woman in the workplace. Angela would be no different. He didn't mix business with pleasure.

He banished the thought and finally replied, "I'm sure you are." Then he walked over to his desk, procured a folder and handed it to her. "Read this. It'll fill you in on the development. Let's plan on putting our heads together on a marketing strategy tomorrow after you've had time to digest it."

Angela nodded and walked toward the door. "And, Daniel?"

"Yes?"

"Thank you for the opportunity."

When Angela returned to her desk, she was still on cloud nine despite Daniel Cobb's stern warning not to get overly confident. This was her biggest sale and a chance to impress him.

Over the last six months Angela had watched every move Daniel made. Though he was charming and suave on the outside, she knew he was cutthroat on the inside. He couldn't have gotten to the top without being a little ruthless. She'd seen him pulverize buyers' and sellers' agents alike to get what he wanted. That's why he was a transactional broker. He worked as a facilitator between the buyer and seller to close the transaction. He didn't owe either party his undivided loyalty. Nonetheless, she'd seen him use the utmost skill, care and diligence in all his transactions, dealing honestly and fairly with all the clients he represented.

He was recently featured in *Miami magazine* as an industry star. Everyone knew who Daniel was, including lots of women. Since she'd arrived six months ago, Angela had seen lots of wannabes sashay into Cobb's offices trying to meet Daniel or have him show them property *personally*. She was sure most of them were either in the market to be a Mrs. or looking for a good time, and Daniel certainly fit the bill.

Angela tried not to notice how handsome Daniel was, but she'd failed miserably. Not only was he irrepressibly charming, but he had killer features: chiseled cheekbones, a broad nose, a strong chin and sumptuously full lips. And those eyes…

His eyes dared any woman to look into them and not

get burned by their dark brown intensity. Angela always made sure not to stare too closely at him for fear she'd get tangled in the web of attraction like so many women before her.

And then there was the body. She was sure there was a vast expanse of steel-toned chest, rock-hard abs and powerful thighs underneath those designer suits he wore. They were enough to make any woman's knees wobbly at the prospect of a passionate encounter with the man. Angela shook her head. She mustn't think that way.

Daniel was her boss and he would remain only her boss, even if he was wearing the heck out of a Tom James suit.

"Angela." Myrna snapped her out of her musings.

"Yes?"

"You interested in going to lunch? Daisy will cover me while we go out."

"I just got back to the office," Angela responded.

"C'mon," Myrna pleaded, "I've been stuck in here all day and I need a break. I can't wait until the day when I can get out of the office and start showing houses."

"All right," Angela conceded, and grabbed the Prada purse that was hanging over her chair. She tossed it over her shoulder and followed the statuesque blonde out of the office, uncaring that she had the attention of the owner of the establishment.

Once they were seated at an open-air bistro facing the bay and enjoying the warm day in early May, Myrna wasted no time getting to the real reason she'd asked Angela to lunch.

"You have to tell me your secret," Myrna stated.

"What secret?"

"How you got Daniel to notice you," Myrna said, sipping on her iced green tea. "I've been trying for months, but he just looks right through me as though I'm not there."

Angela laughed. "As if that were possible." Myrna was gorgeous and she knew it. Every man sitting outside was giving her sideways glances. Was she really so disturbed that Daniel wasn't one of them?

"It is," Myrna said, pushing her Asian salad around on her plate. "I want to be an agent same as you one day, but the state test is god-awful. I've failed twice."

"I've heard it can be difficult," Angela responded, though it hadn't been for her. She'd passed on her initial try and never looked back. Why? Because she'd finally found what she wanted to do in life after floundering in endless jobs for close to a decade. A career that would showcase her brain for business.

"You have no idea," Myrna said. "And when I finally pass, I want Daniel to give me a shot, a real shot at working for him. To see me as something more than just a pretty face to wow clients when they walk through the door."

"Do you really think that's why he hired you?"

"C'mon, Angela," Myrna stated, reaching for her bottle of Evian water. She unscrewed the top and drank liberally. "We both know my looks got me the job. But they won't get me my dream job. You're so lucky."

"Yeah, I guess I am," Angela replied. "But it wasn't always this way."

"What do you mean?"

Angela wasn't about to share her story with Myrna, who was known to gossip in the office. She couldn't tell her that her parents, both academics, saw Angela as a disappointment because she wasn't more like her sister, Denise, who was working on her PhD. "I mean that sometimes you have to start at the bottom and work your way up."

"Is that what you did?" Myrna snorted. "Yet somehow you caught Daniel's eye."

"Not in the way that you mean," Angela said. "He has a new project that he wants me to work on with him."

"And is that all he wants you to work on?"

Angela raised a brow. "What are you talking about?"

"C'mon, you must know Daniel Cobb has a reputation. He's quite the ladies' man, or so I've heard."

"And from *whom* have you heard that?" Angela queried.

Myrna shrugged. "Around. People talk. And word on the street is that Daniel has an aversion to commitment. So all I'm saying is that I hope this venture is on the up-and-up and that you need to be on your guard. A man as suave and charming as Daniel Cobb just might sneak up on you."

Angela sat back in her seat. She highly doubted that. She had her eye on the prize. Getting out of her small yet expensive apartment and into one of the luxurious condos she'd set her sights on two years ago when she'd begun saving. And no man, including Daniel Cobb, was going to get her off her game.

Chapter 2

Daniel eased his red Ferrari up to the valet station outside a fifty-five-story tower in Brickell, Miami's financial district, the following day.

A valet greeted him, relieving him of his keys, and Daniel strode inside the formidable tower to the elevator and pressed the button for the top floor, where he was set to attend the monthly meeting for Prescott George.

Seven years ago, he'd been invited to join the illustrious men's club by the president, Ashton Rollins. In the seventy-five-year history of the organization, no one actually called it Prescott George. They all referred to it as the Millionaire Moguls Club. Why? Because anyone who was anyone knew that the discreet and powerful club only invited old money and a handful of the nouveau riche to join them. That's not to say the Millionaire Moguls didn't give back.

Their motto was From Generation to Generation, Lifting Each Other Up. The club regularly gave college scholarships to needy students and funding to inner-city organizations. It's why Daniel was here today. They were settling on the charity organization that would be the beneficiary of Prescott George's upcoming annual fund-raising gala.

As he stood in the elevator, Daniel was sure there were going to be fireworks in today's meeting between Joshua DeLong, the charity outreach and public relations chair, and Ashton. The two men were like oil and water; they didn't mix. They had numerous differences, not the least of which was the source of their fortunes, and in that regard Daniel compared himself, as well. Ashton was a rich kid who'd been born into money, unlike Daniel, who'd earned his, and Joshua, who, rumor had it, had stolen his fortune. As a corporate raider, Joshua had a way of taking what he wanted, regardless of if it was from the misfortune of others. Still, he was a likable guy with loads of charisma.

And then there was Ashton.

Daniel wasn't Ashton's biggest fan, either, but his animosity went deeper, much deeper, and further back into their shared history.

The *ding* of the elevator indicated they'd reached the top level and Daniel exited. The doors opened into an old boys' club. Or at least that's how Daniel saw it. The wood-paneled walls and leather furniture were certainly of a bygone era and could use some updating. Daniel's mission was to change that.

A beautifully stunning chocolate sister was at the mahogany receptionist desk and greeted him. "Good afternoon, Mr. Cobb. The meeting hasn't yet convened in the conference room." She nodded her head toward the corridor where the rest of the club was gathered.

"Thank you, Tiffany."

"Can I get you anything to drink? A scotch, perhaps?"

Daniel never drank during the day. He liked to keep a cool head. "No, thank you." As he strode down the corridor to the conference room, he noted the prominent portraits of George Rollins and Prescott Owens, the club founders, that lined the walls. Daniel was certain that was one of the reasons Joshua disliked Ashton—because he hadn't earned his title of president. He'd inherited it from his grandfather George and his father, Alexander Rollins.

According to the history books, only a member of the Rollins or Owens families had ever served as its leader. And the old-timers were committed to keeping things that way. But Daniel and Joshua were new-school, nouveau riche and ready to bring the Millionaire Moguls into the twenty-first century.

And the Millionaire Moguls Club would do so kicking and screaming.

Daniel arrived at the conference room to find nearly everyone there. Ashton was at the head of the long rectangular table, and Joshua flanked him on his left, refusing to budge. Daniel smiled. He was sure Ashton would love some breathing room from his nemesis. Daniel took a seat, flanking Ashton to his right.

Comparatively, Ashton and Joshua couldn't look any more different. Ashton appeared every bit the preppy in his Ralph Lauren suit and classic striped tie, while Joshua wore a navy blazer over a white T-shirt and dark jeans. Daniel knew Ashton hated when members didn't look the part, and he suspected Joshua dressed intentionally to get under Ashton's skin.

Ashton used his gavel to bring the meeting to order. Surprisingly, it went much smoother than Daniel had expected. They discussed old business, one item of which was Daniel's. As chair for the anniversary gala it was his job to ensure that finances were in order for the event. Then there was new business. For once, the board members were all in agreement that this year's beneficiary would be The Aunt Penny Foundation, especially after Joshua's compelling pitch on its behalf.

And on cue, Joshua couldn't resist ruffling feathers before the meeting concluded. "I think we should give some thought as to how we capitalize on this for the club—you know, get a little name recognition."

"Of course you would want to capitalize on another person's misfortune," Ashton replied.

Joshua glared at him sideways with those piercing blue eyes. Daniel suspected that with his curly fro, Joshua was of mixed race, but had never asked. "Perhaps capitalizing was the wrong word choice. But we need to take advantage of the positive press this could bring the Millionaire Moguls."

Ashton pointed his finger at him. "First off, we're called Prescott George," he responded. "Second, we keep our charity activities private. We don't give so we can get recognized for it."

"I agree with Ashton," another board member concurred. He was well into his fifties and of the old regime, who were staunchly against change. "We don't give to get praised."

"I'm with Ashton," another member said. "It seems awfully disingenuous."

Daniel rolled his eyes. Of course they all agreed, because no one wanted to go up against a Rollins. The

Rollins family was well-established not only in their organization, but in the community. They were a Miami institution.

"Even if our efforts could help bring more donations to The Aunt Penny Foundation?" Joshua inquired. "Wouldn't it be worth it?"

"Let's table this discussion for another time," Ashton said, effectively ending any further conversation on the matter. Because that's what Ashton did. He was used to getting his way, as his father and his father's father before him.

Daniel was tired of it, and as he glanced at Joshua, he recognized that he was, too. It was just a matter of time before the tensions between the two warring factions of old-timers and new blood came to a head.

Later that afternoon, Angela waited for Daniel's return from his monthly meeting. She'd heard he was a member of the illustrious Millionaire Moguls, and she wasn't surprised. According to *Miami magazine*, his net worth was upward of ten million, and with his flashy digs in Key Biscayne and his sporty Ferrari, she was sure he fit right in with the rich men of Miami.

She wanted to be just like him. And didn't they say that imitation was the sincerest form of flattery? She didn't need to be quite as flashy as Daniel, but she certainly wanted the freedom that came with being independently wealthy. And if she played her cards right, rubbing shoulders with Daniel Cobb just might do it for her.

As if his ears were burning, Daniel strode into the office with equal parts style and arrogance. She watched him check in with Myrna before glancing in her direction. He walked toward her desk purposefully.

"Did you have time to read the prospectus?"

"Yes—" She didn't get another word in because he cut her off.

"Let's go. We're meeting the developer in thirty minutes, and with Miami traffic it's going to be close."

Angela quickly glanced around for her portfolio and purse, flustered as Daniel stared down at his Piaget watch, looking annoyed with her fumbling.

"Ticktock, Angela."

Finding her portfolio underneath a pile of papers, she quickly grabbed it, tossed her purse over her shoulder and followed him out of the office. She gave Myrna a quick wave as they exited.

"Not much notice," Angela replied.

Daniel turned to give her a sideward glance. "If you're expecting our wealthy, overly indulged clients to care one iota about your time, then you're in the wrong business."

The elevator chimed, signaling its arrival. The cab was crowded, but with no time to spare they stepped inside. There was hardly any room so Angela's backside was pressed against the hard wall of Daniel's body. She was extremely uncomfortable with the close proximity and hated that the arresting scent of his cologne filled her senses.

Why did the man have to smell so good?

When one of the occupants from the rear came forward to get off at a lower floor, jostling her, Daniel's muscled arm instantly reached out and circled her middle, preventing her from falling. Angela's breath hitched in her throat at the contact. It was a shock to have Daniel's hands anywhere on her body. When she righted herself, she glanced behind her.

"Th-thank you."

He grinned as if he knew the devastating effect he had on women, including her. "You're welcome."

Angela was thankful when they arrived at the VIP level of the building's garage and disembarked without incident. She followed Daniel to his Ferrari. It was gleaming and shiny and looked like just the kind of toy a playboy like Daniel would drive.

"Buckle up. We need to get to our destination in a hurry," Daniel said as she tried to get into the low-slung car as femininely as possible.

Seconds later, all Angela heard was the screeching of the tires as he sped out of the parking space and zoomed out of the garage.

They arrived at their appointment with minutes to spare. Daniel quickly exited the car, then came around to open her car door and offer her a hand.

She slid hers inside his and noted how warm his hands felt. *Would they feel that way on my body?* Yikes, when had she gone down this path of thinking of Daniel as a man instead of her boss? Myrna. She was going to have to stop listening to the blonde's flights of fancy.

They walked side by side into the building, but again Daniel was ever the gentleman, opening the glass door for her. He led her to the sales office that was next to the entrance. It was light and airy with lots of natural sunlight and bright colors, and it held a scale model of what the building and amenities would look like, including a rooftop deck, a fitness center with a sauna and even a Starbucks.

"Daniel! There you are." A dark-haired Latino man rushed toward him. Similar to Daniel, he was stylishly dressed in a designer suit, and it was clear he had a good barber, because there wasn't a hair out of place.

"Eduardo." Daniel extended his hand. "Good to see you."

Eduardo eyed Angela at his side. "And who did you bring with you? A buyer perhaps for my amazing condo?"

Angela smiled. She was glad she was wearing Dolce & Gabbana today and looked like she *could* afford to buy a place like this.

Daniel gave her a cursory glance. "Afraid not. Eduardo Torres, meet Angela Trainor, one of my agents I'm mentoring. Angela will be working with me on this project."

Eduardo gave him a grin. "I can see why." He eyed Angela from her stilettos to her face. "Eye candy will be good for business."

Angela opened her mouth to tell Mr. Eduardo Torres a thing or two, but Daniel shook his head.

"Come, let's talk." Daniel placed his massive hand on Eduardo's narrow shoulders and started walking toward the table that had the model of the building.

Angela had no choice but to follow behind them. She didn't like how Eduardo made her feel, as if she were irrelevant and only there for show. She was a darn good real estate agent and getting better every day. She would have to assert herself so he saw her as something other than a pretty face.

"When are you going to have the marketing campaign ready?" Eduardo inquired. "It's important that the project make a splash on the market and we maybe get some offers at the launch party."

"Relax, Eduardo," Daniel said in a soft tone to calm the highly charged man. "This isn't my first rodeo." He used Angela's turn of phrase from earlier. "I've steered several projects toward full occupancy before the buildings were built."

"But none of this size," Eduardo responded quickly. "This building will have eighty units. That's a lot to sell in eighteen months."

"And I—correction, we—" Daniel glanced over at Angela and despite herself, her heart fluttered in her chest "—will sell out these units. You've come to the right firm, Eduardo. You just have to give *us* time to come up with the right plan to market to these hip millennials. Trust me, we'll have this place filled in no time."

After Eduardo departed, leaving them alone in the sales office, Daniel turned to her. "This project is a big deal for Cobb Luxury Real Estate."

"And you're going to do great," Angela commented. "I mean, *we're* going to do great."

"You say that like you mean it."

Angela's brow furrowed. "I do mean it. I came here because of your reputation. Everyone's talking about you, Daniel. They know you have your pulse on the real estate market in South Florida. Everyone wants to emulate you, *be* you."

Daniel stood back and regarded her. "Including you?"

Angela locked eyes with his. "Of course. I would imagine you get a thrill out of having all of us lowly peons looking up to the great Daniel Cobb for advice and guidance."

Daniel chuckled. "It's not always easy being at the top. There's a long fall to the bottom."

"Ah, but you're one of the Millionaire Moguls," Angela responded. "With their backing behind you, I'm sure the members alone could buy up this place in a heartbeat."

"So you've heard of us?" There was a smile in his voice.

"Who in Miami hasn't? You're synonymous with wealth and tradition."

Daniel pointed his finger. "See, that's the image I no longer want for the organization. It's time to bring them forward to the new millennium."

"And you're just the man to do that?"

"One of them," Daniel said. "Speaking of the Millionaire Moguls, I'd like you to join me for a dinner we're having on Friday night."

Angela cleared her throat. Had she heard him correctly? Was he asking her out? "Join you?"

"Yes," Daniel replied, "I think it would be great for you to meet some of the influential members of the organization. Could be potential clients for you. What do you say?"

There was no way she was turning down an invitation to rub elbows with the rich and famous. She gave him her most dazzling smile. "Count me in."

Why in the hell had he just asked Angela to join him at the Millionaire Moguls monthly dinner? It was usually reserved for members and their spouses or significant others, of which Angela was neither. Yet there was something about her that Daniel liked. She was smart and confident and spoke her mind. He liked that in a woman. Not to mention the fact that she was hot as hell.

Of course, he had no intention of going there with Angela. He was just curious to learn more about her. It had been a while since a woman had piqued his interest. Made him want to see what was under the hood rather than just admiring the package. And Lord knew, Angela was one helluva package.

Take today for instance. She'd shown poise and professionalism when Eduardo treated her disrespectfully by speaking solely to Daniel even though he'd told the

Cuban that Angela would work on the project with him. Instead of reacting, she'd quietly stood by and when the moment was right, she'd interjected herself into the conversation with pointed information on the Miami market. Slowly, he'd seen Eduardo warm up to the notion that this beautiful woman had a head on her shoulders.

He, too, had admired the authority with which she spoke. It's why he'd uncharacteristically asked out an employee, something he never did. But she didn't need to know that. All she would think was that he was her mentor and showing her the ropes.

"Excellent," Daniel commented on her acceptance of his offer. "I'll swing by and pick you up at your place."

"Oh, that's not necessary. I'll just meet you at the office."

He frowned. Even though she was his employee, he always liked to escort his women home. "Are you sure?"

"Absolutely." Angela smiled at him.

Once Angela made it to her apartment in Coconut Grove that evening, she kicked off her shoes at the door and plopped herself on the microsuede sofa. It had been a long day, made even longer by the fact that she'd been wearing four-inch heels. Lying back, Angela rubbed her aching feet and thought about her day.

She was thrilled that Daniel had finally taken her under his wing to assist him with selling this new development. She'd been waiting for the opportunity when she could show him that he hadn't made a mistake in hiring her.

What she hadn't been expecting was Daniel to ask her out. Oh sure, he disguised it as a business dinner, saying she was merely joining him at an event for an organization he was active in and it would broaden her contacts. But from all angles that she could see, it was a date. She would be his companion for the evening, when she was sure other men would be bringing their spouses or partners.

Should she be concerned that they were mixing work and pleasure? Angela didn't think so, nor did she care. She wanted the chance to meet other affluent men and their wives who might need a real estate agent. If she played her cards right, the business that might come her way would be worth the time spent with Daniel.

Not that it would be a hardship to be his date for the evening. Daniel was a fine specimen. He was the type of man a woman could easily get addicted to if she let herself. But romance wasn't on Angela's agenda. Or so she told herself. She needed to wow. To impress.

Rising from the sofa, she knew just the outfit she'd wear.

It was a sleek one-shoulder black cocktail dress with a crossover skirt that gave a hint of side slit without being too revealing. She would pair it with some classic peep-toe black pumps and wear her hair in a loose chignon. She would be stylish and sophisticated and would fit in with the other women come Friday night.

Chapter 3

On Friday evening, Daniel ventured upstairs to his office, opting to check a few emails while he waited for Angela. Although he liked to play hard and made time for extracurricular activities, he was a notorious workaholic. Plus, he was trying his best to not think of tonight as a date.

But as soon as he glanced up and saw Angela standing in the doorway, he knew he'd made a grave miscalculation. He was transfixed, staring at her with open admiration.

Tall and sleek, Angela looked radiant. Slightly tousled hair. Flawless skin with just a touch of blush. Warm brown eyes. Perfectly arched eyebrows. She was a vision in a black dress with one silky shoulder exposed to his view, along with a long expanse of leg that led to spiky heeled sandals.

He swallowed. "You clean up nice," he managed to say, trying to find his footing in the situation.

Her brow furrowed. "Uh, thanks."

Had she been expecting a different reaction? If he wasn't her employer, he would have responded differently, but tonight he had to remember his hands-off policy when it came to employees.

But Angela was going to make that policy hard to follow.

He rose from his chair. "Ready to go?"

She motioned him forward. "Lead the way."

Daniel walked toward her, and when he did he caught a hint of raspberry and...was that vanilla? The scent was fun and flirty and he couldn't resist smiling. Or appreciating all her curves now that he was mere inches away from her.

"You look pretty good yourself," she commented.

"Uh, thanks," he said, mimicking her earlier response. He offered her his arm, which Angela accepted, and they headed for the elevator. He'd arranged for a driver to take them to the restaurant.

During the ride over, he hazarded a glance in Angela's direction and caught sight of several inches of thigh, thanks to the way she'd positioned herself in the vehicle. He immediately turned his attention to the window to stare outside, reprimanding himself for looking at Angela like a beautiful woman.

Blessedly, the ride from Cobb's offices to the restaurant was quick. Daniel didn't have to worry what would happen if he touched her, because the valet was there to help her out of the car. He was thankful because despite the fact that they'd maintained a polite conversation on the ride, he found himself on edge. Daniel exited and joined Angela, leading her toward the private rooms the Millionaire Moguls had procured for the evening.

"Daniel." Tyson Williams, another member, caught them outside the dining room. "And who is this lovely lady you've brought with you this evening?"

Before he could answer, Angela offered her hand. "Angela, Angela Trainor," she responded. "Daniel and I work together at Cobb Luxury Real Estate." She glanced at Daniel, giving him an arresting smile that was like a punch in his gut. Why was he having such a visceral physical response to this woman?

"Really, Cobb? You couldn't find a date, so you asked out one of your own people?"

Daniel snorted. "Watch it, Tyson. Otherwise, I'll beat you in another game of racquetball and have you wishing I'd shown you mercy."

Tyson pointed at Daniel. "See this guy?" he asked Angela. "If I were you I'd be careful."

Angela was well aware that she had to be extremely careful around Daniel, because he looked downright dangerous tonight. The man was every bit as dangerously sleek as a powerful panther.

When she'd arrived at the office to meet him earlier, she hadn't been surprised to find him hunched over his computer tapping away at the keys. She had, however, been surprised at how attractive she'd found him as he'd walked toward her. His movements might have been smooth and relaxed, but there was an inherent strength and power in Daniel that Angela recognized and responded to.

She'd sucked in a deep breath when he'd slid past her

in the doorway of his office, and all she'd been able to manage was, "You look pretty good yourself."

Totally unoriginal.

But then again, who could blame her? She'd been face-to-face with the man, able to see all his features from his dark eyes to his extremely appealing mouth.

"Angela." His smooth voice snagged her attention from her reverie and she looked at him beside her. He motioned her into a room that was already full of people. She estimated at least a dozen tables had been arranged for dinner. Angela instantly recognized several men, including the mayor and a city council member. "Come, I'd like to introduce you around."

Daniel introduced her first to Ashton Rollins, the president of Prescott George. Angela wasn't surprised a Rollins led the organization. They were well established in the community and had been for years. The Rollins estate on Fisher Island was even mentioned in the tour she'd taken when she decided to move here.

Surprisingly Ashton came alone.

Angela was shocked that some socialite hadn't snagged a catch like him. She, however, wasn't interested. Despite the appeal of his millions, he was a little too stiff for Angela's taste. He wore a classic suit and silver tie, and didn't have Daniel's same pizzazz or style.

To her delight, Daniel introduced her to the governor and his wife, along with a few other affluent members of the community, before he eventually went off to talk to several of his friends, leaving Angela to fend for herself. She opted for a glass of wine and was standing in line at the open bar when a wife she'd encountered earlier commented from behind her.

"And how did you manage to land a playboy like Daniel?" the woman inquired.

Angela spun around. "Excuse me?"

"Oh, do tell," the woman gushed. "It can't have been easy gaining Daniel Cobb's attention. Several of us—" she motioned to a group of at least half a dozen women who were gathered in a semicircle a short distance away "—have been trying to set him up for years with our girlfriends and have never been successful. What's your secret?"

Of course they would assume she was his girlfriend, because that's who wealthy men brought as their dinner dates to events such as these. But Angela had to clear the air. She didn't want to be disingenuous. "Daniel and I aren't dating."

The woman touched her chest. "You aren't?"

"No, we're colleagues at his real estate firm."

"So you're *single*?"

The way she said it made Angela feel like it was a dirty word among these women.

"I had no idea," the woman muttered and quickly rushed off to speak with the other women in the group.

"Ma'am, what would you like?" the bartender inquired. It was Angela's turn to order.

"Chardonnay, please."

Angela glanced toward the group of women and several of them were either outright glaring at her or giving her the stink eye. Was it really so horrible that she was single? What did they think she was going to do? Go after one of their husbands?

She was not interested in being anyone's side piece. For her, it was all or nothing.

* * *

"Who's the vixen you brought with you?" Joshua De-Long asked Daniel when he finally escaped a torturous conversation with an older member of the organization.

Daniel raised a brow. "Vixen?" He didn't like Joshua's word choice, but at least his friend had deigned to dress appropriately for the evening in trousers and a suit jacket sans tie. But then again, had Daniel ever seen Joshua in a tie?

"Yeah," Joshua said from his side. "She's pretty hot and all the women here are green with envy. Look around." He inclined his head to two distinctive groups of women that were staring at Angela as if she were a leopard about to steal their young.

But Daniel wasn't worried. "She can handle herself. I wouldn't have brought her to Cobb Luxury Real Estate if I thought some insecure socialites could get the better of her."

"It's like that, huh?"

"Yeah, she has some skills. Skills that just need some refinement."

"And you're just the man to do that?" Joshua queried.

"Get your head out of the gutter, my friend," Daniel said. "Angela's my employee, nothing more." And with that, he moved in her direction.

But before he could make it there, Angela had already headed to one group of women who were giving her the evil eye. She didn't seem in the least bit put off by their less-than-receptive greeting. He thought about going over to save her, but instead stood back and watched.

Five minutes later, Angela had the women laughing and talking and pretty much eating out of her hand. She'd handled their animosity and their concern that she might be a threat to any one of their marriages with gracefulness.

Daniel was proud not only to have her on his staff, but to have her on his arm tonight.

He walked toward them. "Ladies," he said as he inclined his head toward the women. "Mind if I steal her away?"

"Certainly." One of the other wives beamed at him.

Once they were away from the group, Daniel whispered in her ear. "You handled that marvelously."

She gave him an incredulous look. "Did you doubt that I would?"

Daniel shook his head. "Not at all. You know how to handle people."

"I do," she replied. "You included."

Angela didn't know what made her say it, but she'd definitely been flirting. She'd let Daniel know in no uncertain terms that she could take him on any time of day. But was she really ready to do that? Theirs was a working relationship that tonight had crossed the line. Would there be any going back?

Since the dinner was about to begin and everyone was finding a seat, they did the same. Daniel and Angela sat at a table with eight other people. She hadn't met the man immediately to her right and Daniel wasted no time introducing them.

"Angela, I'd like you to meet my good friend, Joshua DeLong. Joshua is a relatively new member to Prescott George."

"Nice to meet you, Joshua." Angela offered her hand, which Joshua pumped enthusiastically while looking her straight in the eye. She liked him and those blue eyes of his immediately.

Joshua DeLong was certainly the heartbreaker type with those baby blues, but at least he hadn't sized her up like he wanted to take her to bed like some of the married men had tonight. A few wives had a right to be worried. If the wrong single woman had been here tonight and not Angela, there might have been some deals made that had nothing to do with business.

"Joshua is our charity outreach and public relations chair," Daniel said.

"And what does that entail?" Angela inquired.

"Are you familiar with Prescott George?" Joshua asked.

"I am."

"Every year we support a deserving foundation or charity, and they benefit from our fund-raising proceeds."

"That's wonderful," Angela responded. "Do you already have this year's recipient in mind?"

Her enthusiastic response to the project caused Joshua to smile. "Sure do. Ever heard of The Aunt Penny Foundation?"

"No, tell me about it."

"The Aunt Penny Foundation provides mentoring and counseling to high school seniors who are in need of assistance. I'll be meeting with their representative shortly to go over the details."

"Sounds like an excellent organization to support," Angela said.

Joshua jabbed his thumb in Daniel's direction. "I like this girl. She's a keeper."

That's exactly how Daniel felt. Even more so as the evening progressed. Since Angela had been at the firm, they'd rarely discussed anything personal. And with his laser focus on work, he hadn't given her much thought other than recognizing she was a beautiful woman.

But tonight, it was like he was seeing her for the first time.

Throughout the four-course dinner, Daniel and Angela had their heads together in private conversation.

"So you're from here?"

"No," Angela replied, "my folks live here. My father, Eric Trainor, is a professor at University of Miami."

"And your mother?"

"Ella, she's a high school principal. And my sister, Denise, is in graduate school studying for her PhD in education. So as you can see, all the members of my family are academics. My parents wish I'd be more like my sister. They find it hard to believe that I can make a living being a real estate agent given my history."

"Do tell," Daniel said, leaning in closer.

Angela turned to face him. Sitting so close to Daniel, she could smell just a hint of his aftershave and it filled her senses. Daniel was impossible to ignore. He was the kind of man who drew attention, and that's exactly what he was doing to her this very moment. She normally didn't speak about her family to anyone, but tonight she was being more open than she had been in a long time.

"I'm sure I'm not the first teenager to want to take off for parts unknown, see the world." She shrugged and reached for her wineglass, which somehow was refilled every time she sat it down.

She took a sip.

"Your parents didn't approve?"

She shook her head. "No, they thought I should stay in college, but I wanted to live a little, see the world. And

I did. I ended up bumming around Europe for a couple of years, working odd jobs, until finally coming back to the States."

"But you didn't ever go back to school?"

"No. I'd already seen what it was like to live on my own and didn't want the regimented lifestyle that being in college required. And so I went from one job to the next, until I worked as a receptionist at a real estate agency."

"Same as Myrna."

"Indeed. I learned a lot and realized that I had what it took and I could make the same sort of commissions I helped the broker and agents make. So I signed up for real estate class immediately. Passed the state test on my first try because I think I was finally passionate about something other than men, clothes and shoes."

A smile creased his face. "Are you a shopaholic?"

Angela held up her hand. "Guilty as charged, and I have the closet bursting at the seams to prove it. But I've since calmed down because there are some goals I want to achieve."

Daniel leaned back. "Talk to me about them. What are your long-term plans?"

Angela beamed. "To not only become a successful agent, but to one day open my own agency, same as you."

"Quite lofty goals."

"But not impossible ones," Angela responded quickly.

"You're stuck in the twentieth century!" A loud voice boomed through the room, interrupting their conversation.

Daniel knew the owner of that voice.

Joshua.

He glanced behind him and saw that Joshua had indeed left the table. And Daniel didn't need to guess who he was yelling at.

Ashton.

Daniel wiped his mouth with the napkin from his lap. "Excuse me for just a moment," he said, and quickly left the private dining area.

He found Joshua and Ashton both standing outside the open doors. "Do you have any idea that everyone can hear you?" Daniel snapped, closing the double doors behind him.

"I'm trying to explain to this dinosaur that he's stuck in the Stone Age," Joshua replied. "We need to be capitalizing on all the positive press that a social media blitz and good press could do for The Aunt Penny Foundation. Hell, for us, too, but he refuses to see it." Joshua paced back and forth as he ranted.

"There is no such thing as good publicity," Ashton replied, calmly. "Not in this day and age. Are you so blinded by your animosity toward me that you can't see that? Prescott George is about lifting people up. All the press knows how to do is bring people down. Furthermore, now isn't the time to be discussing this."

"You have to know how to spin publicity," Joshua replied, "which clearly you don't but I do. I'm a master puppeteer at getting the press to report exactly what I want them to."

"Like the fact that you steal other people's money?" Ashton said. "Did you give them that tidbit, too?"

Joshua steamed beside him and Daniel thought he might deck Ashton, but instead he turned to Daniel. "Tell him." He pointed to Ashton. "Tell him I'm right."

Both pairs of eyes turned to Daniel. He hated that Joshua was putting him on the spot like this.

"I think both of you are upset right now and need to let cooler heads prevail," Daniel returned. "Ashton is right. Now isn't the right time to discuss this." He watched a smirk cross Ashton's face. "But I think Joshua's suggestion merits further discussion."

"You're agreeing with him?" Ashton wasn't happy that Daniel wasn't taking his side. It was clear that Ashton was not a fan of Joshua's. Daniel had long since suspected that he thought Joshua was an interloper who'd smooth-talked his way into the organization. It certainly had been one of the younger members who'd invited Joshua to join Prescott George. If Ashton had his way, Daniel was sure there would be only legacy members. But it was a new dawn and a new day, and Ashton was soon going to realize that Prescott George had to change with the times.

"I'm keeping the peace," Daniel said. "As leaders of the organization, you both need to go back in that room and show them there is no friction."

Ashton huffed, but opened the doors and walked back in while Joshua fumed outside.

"Why do you always try to play mediator?" he countered to Daniel. "Eventually you'll have to choose sides. Mine or his."

Daniel rolled his eyes. "How about neither?" he responded, and turned on his heel and walked back into the room.

When he returned to the table, Angela asked, "Is everything okay?"

He nodded. "Yes, everything is fine. Just a difference of opinion. Sometimes we men get rather loud."

But Daniel feared this wasn't the end of Joshua's beef with Ashton; he suspected that the stakes were about to get significantly higher.

* * *

His mind was elsewhere, Angela thought when Daniel returned to the table. She tried reengaging him in conversation, but it was clear that the night was over. She supposed she should be thankful that the electricity she'd been feeling earlier in the evening had cooled. She'd felt stirred by Daniel, and that would never do. He was her boss who'd asked her to accompany him to a business dinner. She mustn't forget that.

As the evening came to a close, Angela and Daniel said their goodbyes, and shortly after they were seated back in the town car.

"Would you like us to drop you home?" he asked her.

"I left my car at the office, remember?"

"Oh, of course. I'm sorry," he apologized. "I've been a bit distracted this evening."

"It's fine."

"It's not. It was incredibly rude of me. Allow me to make it up to you by following you home."

"Follow me home?" Angela's heart began hammering in her chest. "That's not necessary. I've got it."

They drifted into a comfortable silence until the driver eased the town car next to hers in the garage. Daniel requested he keep the engine idling and turned to face her. "I had a really good time tonight."

"So did I. Thanks again." Angela didn't wait for his response and quickly opened the passenger door. She wasn't sure what was going on between them, but she wasn't sticking around to find out.

She was in her car within seconds and was about to pull out when she saw Daniel had rolled down the rear window and was motioning to her. Sighing, Angela lowered the window. "Yes?"

"I'm following you home."

"I told you that's not necessary. I'm a big girl."

"You are, but I'd feel more comfortable, so we're just going to follow behind you."

Angela rolled her eyes. She didn't want Daniel to see where she lived. Her apartment building was ordinary and certainly nothing like the luxury ones they sold. Now he would know that she was merely acting and dressing like she was one of them. He'd see she was a fraud. But she had no choice because he'd already raised his window.

When she arrived at her apartment building thirty minutes later, Daniel was still behind her in the town car. She sighed when he exited the vehicle and turned off the engine.

Oh Lord!

He came around to the driver's side of her car and opened her door. She exited, but all she could do was stand there, holding on to the door. For what—support? Or to escape back inside so she wouldn't be faced with the potent magnetism that exuded from Daniel's every pore?

"You really didn't have to do this," she began, but he placed an index finger over her lips. Angela sucked in a deep breath at the light contact.

"I understand why you didn't want me to come, Angela, but it's nothing to be embarrassed about." Daniel glanced up at the building. "Before my parents divorced, I grew up in a middle-class community. It was a far cry from where I live now."

"Yeah, well, some of us can't live as upscale as all that," Angela responded.

"I know that. So be proud of who you are and where

you come from." He reached out and tucked a wayward curl behind her ear. Doing so brought his sensual mouth entirely too close to her own. "It's made you who you are."

She glanced up at him. And in that moment, she wanted him to kiss her. Oh, how she wanted it. She would instantly surrender if he tried.

Instead his hands moved from her hair to slide across her cheek. "Get inside safe and I'll see you at the office on Monday. Nine o'clock sharp."

All Angela could do was nod and walk with leaden feet to the door of her apartment building, feeling as if she'd been kissed even though he'd barely even touched her. And that could only mean one thing. Trouble.

Chapter 4

On Monday Daniel was out of sorts. As much fun as he'd had with Angela on Friday, he wanted their return to the office to be business as usual, because he understood those parameters. However, that was hard to do because his mind kept wandering to how good Angela looked last night and how great she'd smelled when he'd been standing close to her after accompanying her home.

He'd wanted to kiss her. Badly.

His libido had even demanded it, straining in his trousers at just how fine the woman looked. And if he'd made just the slightest overture, turned on his signature charm, she could have been his.

But he hadn't crossed the line.

If he went with his heart's desire, which was to learn more about Angela, he risked problems at the office. But practicing restraint was a lot harder to do than preaching it, especially when Daniel had told Angela that he'd mentor her and that she could accompany him to high-level client meetings.

One of them was a new listing for an eight-bedroom, six-bath waterfront estate on Sunny Isles. The sellers were just the right mix of privileged wealth that Daniel knew Angela needed to be exposed to. In addition to co-brokering with him on the downtown Miami development, Angela would see in person what it would take to sell a development from start to finish.

But he'd promised her he'd take her under his wing, and he was a man of his word.

After some off-site meetings, he returned to the office on Monday afternoon to pick up paperwork for his next appointment and made a beeline for Angela's office. She waved him in, glancing up from her computer screen.

"Hey, there," she said, "how are you? How's your day been?"

Daniel was jolted by just how different Angela looked today. She was back to her usual work attire of a sleeveless fuchsia silk blouse tied at the neck and a black pencil skirt, but no less sexy than she'd been on Friday.

"Busy," Daniel replied, "and about to get even busier. I have a listing appointment at four on Sunny Isles. Care to join me?"

"Sure, just give me a minute. I'll meet you in the lobby."

A few minutes later, Daniel was leaning against the edge of the reception counter chatting with Myrna when Angela came toward him. He stood upright as she approached, desire instantly surging through him when he noticed her long, shapely legs emphasized by a pair of strappy heels. He willed the hard throb of his desire to disappear, but it didn't. His attention was focused so entirely on her sleek body that he ignored Myrna. Instead, he headed swiftly to the door to open it and Angela slid right past him, allowing him to catch sight of her tight bottom as she walked ahead of him.

"So tell me about the estate and the seller," Angela said when Daniel met her at the elevator bank just as the doors were opening. They both stepped inside, but when he opened his mouth to speak he realized just how close she was standing to him. His gaze traveled from the elegant line of her neck to the curve of her shoulders to the smooth, silky strands of hair that hung generously down her back. Angela had returned to the boundaries of their previous encounters, and that was just fine with him. He needed to get his head back on business.

He blinked rapidly and then finally answered her. "Well, it's a seven-thousand-square-foot two-story home that sits on the water and has a private dock. Not to mention there's a spa, a gym and a gorgeous infinity pool with a large outdoor entertaining area."

She smiled. "Impressive. Have you determined a listing price?" Angela asked once he'd finished describing the house and they'd made it to the garage. This time she didn't ask whether she should get in his sports car; she just slid in and buckled up.

"No, but I'm hoping to convince them that seven point five is the right price." He roared the Ferrari to life and exited the garage.

"Are they thinking of more?"

Daniel nodded. "They would love eight million, but the comps in the market aren't supporting it. So I'll talk them off the ledge. They are motivated to sell and don't want it to sit on the market."

"Wise move."

* * *

Angela did her best to keep the conversation focused on selling the Sunny Isles home, but it wasn't easy. She hazarded a glance Daniel's way when his eyes were on the road. He was dressed in a linen suit that was exquisitely cut and showed off the hard muscles she suspected were underneath it. She marveled at the size of his large masculine hands wrapped around the wheel. Sitting beside him right now, Angela was very aware of him.

She'd felt it Friday night, too. Felt the pull of desire between them, but had blown it off as the excitement of the evening. But now? Today? There was no excuse for the way she was feeling. Daniel was off-limits to her and she knew that. But that hadn't stopped her mind from wondering what it would be like to feel his incredibly full lips on her.

Feel the heat of his skin.

Touch him all over.

Their short drive to Sunny Isles went faster than Angela expected, and she was happy to escape the confines of the sporty car. As she exited, Daniel was right there to grasp her hand.

"Thank you." Angela managed to step out onto somewhat shaky legs. Because that's exactly what Daniel's touch did to her. It made her slightly weak in the knees.

They walked together to the impressive front door of the home and Daniel pressed the doorbell. An older woman with flaming red hair and a bright smile greeted them dressed in a colorful print tunic and flowing white pants.

"Daniel, darling," she drawled with a hint of a Southern accent, "please come in."

"Thank you, Mrs. Wilson," Daniel replied as he stepped inside the foyer and Angela followed him. Once inside, he turned to her. "I'd like you to meet my associate Angela Trainor. She'll be partnering with me on this listing."

The woman's brow rose. "Partner? I thought *you* would be representing us."

"And I will be," Daniel responded softly. "I'm mentoring Angela on larger listings such as yours. Let me assure you, you will have *my* expertise at the helm."

A smile returned to her face and Angela tried not to be offended. She knew she wasn't as experienced as Daniel, but the disappointment on Mrs. Wilson's face made it clear that she expected Daniel, and nothing less than the best would do.

"Come, let me show you around," Mrs. Wilson said as she began walking down the corridor.

"And where is Mr. Wilson?" Daniel asked.

"Oh, he'll be joining us as soon as he finishes his business call."

"Of course, lead the way."

Mrs. Wilson showed them the main level of the home, and it was nothing short of spectacular. The Mediterranean home with its whitewashed walls and red tile roof felt open and spacious. Then again, Angela should have known that Daniel represented only exclusive listings.

Eventually, Mrs. Wilson left them to their own devices and Daniel and Angela were able to walk the grounds at their leisure. Their first stop was the private dock.

"What are your thoughts on marketing strategy?" Angela inquired. She could already see the wheels in his mind turning.

Daniel rubbed his square chin. "I'll bring in Elyse to handle staging. Then we'll have to get some new photos of the property showcasing this." He opened his arms, motioning to the stunning water view.

"And the opening?"

"Has to be big," Daniel said. "It has to make a splash. Out here on the terrace with nothing but the best food and drink. Then I'm thinking maybe even some kind of entertainment, like a well-known artist."

Angela's eyes grew wide. "Really? You have that kind of pull?"

"The name Prescott George does."

"A private concert will certainly get attention."

Daniel pointed to her. "That's exactly what we need."

Later, after they'd said goodbye to Mrs. Wilson—since her husband never materialized—Daniel threw her a curveball.

"Would you be interested in attending a Heat game with me on Friday? I have floor seats to the playoff game against the Charlotte Hornets," Daniel said. "I'm taking a buyer I've been trying to woo."

"That must have cost you a mint," Angela murmured. And the minute she said it, she wished she could take it back. It wasn't her place to comment on Daniel's finances or how he chose to run his business.

Instead of saying anything to her, he laughed. "Yeah, it did." Then he told her about the client, Alejandro Rivera. "I've been trying to get his business for some time. He owns homes in Chicago, New York, Dallas and LA. Basically every major metropolitan area. Every time he's in town, I always try to meet up with him for drinks, dinner, tennis, whatever opportunity I can find to get myself in the door. Yet his business has escaped me."

"He's playing hard to get."

"Yes, which is why Friday night is very important. I'm hoping to finally convince him to sign with Cobb."

"And you're hoping a little eye candy will help seal

the deal?" Angela mused aloud. She wasn't unaware of her appearance. Men found her attractive. Desired her, even. She'd seen it. Felt it. Except Daniel was doing his best to dismiss his attraction. If he found it so easy to play cool and unaffected, so could she. At least that's what she told herself.

"You're a fantastic agent," Daniel commented, looking sideways at her.

"But it can't hurt to have a pair of legs with you."

Her words caused Daniel's eyes to momentarily stray from the road and travel from her feet, up her legs and her thighs. From his half smile she could tell he liked everything he saw. His heated perusal caused Angela's pulse to throb, and her breasts thrust forward in the satin bra she wore, making her nipples scream to be touched. Did Daniel even know how hot he was making her with just one glance? Had he noticed her nipples pucker at his gaze?

"No, it can't, and you have one mighty fine pair," he finally murmured.

He shouldn't have said that. But how could he not? Angela had a killer pair of smooth, sexy legs that went on for miles, and he was not as oblivious to her as he was letting on. He wanted her. His gaze had caught the tiny peaks of her nipples against her blouse, and he wished like hell that he could tongue them. His policy of not cavorting with his employees prevented him from acting on his desire.

"Why, thank you, Daniel," Angela replied with a grin. "I didn't think you'd noticed."

"Oh, I noticed," he answered honestly just as he pulled his vehicle into the parking spot inside their office building. He'd noticed everything about her, from the curve of her hips to how long her legs were. He kept the engine idling, but shifted in his seat to face her. Her lips were parted. For what? His kiss?

"Well, I'll see you tomorrow, then," Angela said, opening her door. "Oh, and Friday. Where shall I meet you? At the arena?"

"No. I've arranged for a limo service for the evening, so I'll pick you up at your place," Daniel stated, opening the driver's-side door.

"Th-that's really not necessary. I can meet you there."

He raised his eyes to hers. "It's no trouble. I'll pick you up at six. We'll have dinner at the arena before the game."

"All right." Before he could get out another word, she was exiting the passenger seat.

Daniel was happy for it. He'd had a hard time focusing on driving thanks to the view of her legs in that skirt. Just thinking of how the material stretched over her tight bottom had caused his erection to spring forward in his trousers. But it wasn't all one-sided. Angela did flirt with him. He suspected the attraction simmering between them was about to bubble over.

Angela stared at her backside in the cheval mirror in her bedroom on Friday night. She knew it was a bold move, but she loved how the red leather skinny jeans made her bum look. And would Daniel love it, as well? Though she would never admit if questioned, she had dressed with him in mind tonight. She'd opted for sexy without trying too hard by covering the leather jeans with a white silk button-down shirt and black pointy-toed heels. She jazzed up her outfit with dangling gold chains around her neck, gold hoops adorning her ears and chunky bangles around her wrists.

Overall, she was pleased with the results. Daniel would be able to see she had curves, but they weren't all on display. She was just swiping some lip gloss on when her cell phone rang.

It was her mother.

Angela sighed. She wasn't in the mood for a parental chat right now, but she answered brightly anyway. "Hi, Mama. I was just running out."

"Surely you have time for your mother."

Guilt. Why did her mother always have that effect on her? She hadn't lived at home since she was nineteen and had struck out to travel abroad in Europe. So why did she always feel she was letting her mother down?

"Of course, Mama. We can talk while I finish getting ready." Angela tucked the phone in the crook of her ear and began applying a thick coat of mascara to her eyelashes.

"Where are you headed to at this hour? I would think you'd be winding down after a long week."

"Not tonight. I'm going to a Miami Heat game for work."

Her mother chuckled. "Sounds less like work and more like play."

Angela disliked the disapproving tone in her mother's voice, but she wasn't surprised by it. The Trainors thought that Angela's career as a real estate agent wasn't a real job. How could she be successful by showing homes all day?

"It's a little bit of both. My boss and I are taking a prospective client out for dinner and a game. He's hoping to wine and dine him so he'll sign with our firm."

"I'm sure that's how the game is played in big business. One hand greases another," her mother replied.

Her mother just couldn't resist a put-down.

"Did you want something, Mama?"

"Your sister is going to be coming home in a week for the summer while she's working on her PhD. I thought it would be a great idea if we planned a welcome-home dinner."

"Denise hasn't been gone that long." Five months, if Angela recalled.

"I know, but we haven't seen her all year. And it's not like we see you much now since you started this new position."

Angela glanced in the mirror. Her eyes said it all. She'd used her new job as an excuse to avoid visiting her family. She just hadn't wanted to hear that she didn't measure up to her educated baby sister.

"Mama, I told you how dog-eat-dog it is in the real estate business. I have to stay focused and get my name out there."

"I know that, Angela, but your dad and I miss you girls. And we would love to have the entire family together."

"All right, all right. Just tell me where and when."

After getting the details and finally hanging up with her mother, Angela barely had time to grab her clutch purse and throw a few items in before her buzzer was ringing. Glancing at her watch, she saw it was 6:00 p.m. Daniel was on time.

When she arrived downstairs, a chauffeur was waiting beside the limousine. Angela didn't think the display of wealth was necessary, but she didn't mind enjoying the benefits tonight.

"Good evening, ma'am." The driver tipped his hat to her as he opened the door.

Angela climbed inside and was greeted by the sight of Daniel lounging on the backseat. "Hello," she said.

"Hello, yourself. Have a seat." There wasn't much room for her as his large frame took up most of the seat, but he patted the cushion beside him.

It was going to be impossible to ignore Daniel with him sitting so close. He was the kind of man who dominated his surroundings no matter where he was. In the confines of a car, he could be devastating. But what could she do? Reluctantly, Angela slid in next to him. "Where's Alejandro?"

Daniel chuckled, revealing an even set of gleaming white teeth along with a brilliant smile that made Angela's toes curl in her heels. "Wouldn't you know, Alejandro canceled on me at the last minute? Claimed he got unavoidably detained in Brazil and never made it to Miami."

"That's a shame. I know how much you wanted to pitch the business."

Daniel shrugged. "Another opportunity will arise."

"So…" Angela let the word dangle in the air. "It's just the two of us, then?"

He turned to her with a devilish grin. "It is indeed. I hope you don't have a problem with that."

"Oh no." Angela shook her head furiously. "Of—of course not, it's just that…"

"Just that what?"

"It kind of makes this a date."

"Yeah, it kind of does."

Chapter 5

Daniel didn't mind in the slightest that Alejandro had canceled their plans for tonight. Why? Because it gave him a legitimate excuse to spend the evening with Angela. Not that he needed one. Whatever Daniel wanted, he went after with gusto.

But he was in uncharted territory, given their working relationship. Yet for once, he was willing to take a risk and see where the night led, instead of being the good guy. Look what it had cost him. Mia. If he'd made his feelings known sooner, perhaps… He shook his head. There was no sense looking backward at the past. He could only look at what was in front of him right now.

When the passenger-side door of the limo opened, Angela exited, and Daniel felt his shaft swell to life. How the hell was he going to get through the night if the mere sight of her curvy backside had him horny?

Very gingerly, he thought as he got out of the vehicle.

The chauffeur dropped them off at the door to the VIP area where Daniel produced his floor tickets on his smartphone. While security checked Angela's clutch, another staff member slipped a wristband onto Daniel's wrist and waited for Angela. When they were checked in, Daniel surprised himself and Angela by grasping her hand and leading her down the hall.

Her hand was small and petite, much like Mia's, but her body was curvier. Killed at twenty-one, Mia had never had a chance to fully develop into her womanhood.

Darn! He hated that his past kept resurfacing tonight. What was it about Angela that brought the memories to life? Or perhaps he wasn't as over the loss more than a decade later as he thought he was?

"We're in the back of the house," Angela surmised as they walked down the corridor. "You didn't pull any punches to impress Alejandro, did you?"

Daniel shook his head. "My goal was to show him I know luxury and the finer things in life. During half-time, I'd even procured us cigars in the owner's lounge, but…" His voice trailed off.

"You don't think I can handle a cigar with the big boys?" she teased.

He raised an eyebrow. "Can you?"

"Why don't you try me?"

Daniel laughed. "I just bet you can." He liked her bravado and that she wasn't backing down from a challenge, but he doubted she'd ever smoked a cigar in her life, much less a fine Cuban cigar like the ones they had in the owner's lounge. But he certainly gave her props for bluffing.

"I have a surprise first, though," Daniel said as he led her through the corridor and toward the arena.

"What are we doing?" Angela asked when he walked up to security, pulled out a special badge and was allowed entry right onto the floor where the Heat warmed up.

"Just a little meet and greet," Daniel said. "C'mon."

A Miami Heat promotional staffer dressed in a team jersey approached them. "Daniel Cobb, good to see you, my man." He gave Daniel a handshake.

"You, as well."

"I really appreciate you hooking up the boys at the community center."

"Of course," Daniel said. "Prescott George is committed to helping those in need."

The staff member shook his head. "Yeah, yeah, don't give me the spiel. You didn't have to give ten thousand dollars of your own money to the cause."

"It's the least I could do."

"Well, it was appreciated. Are you and your lady ready to meet some of the players?"

Daniel turned to Angela and noticed she'd raised a brow at his use of the words *your lady*, but she remained silent. "Oh yeah, let's do it."

Angela couldn't believe how warm, friendly and downright accommodating Daniel was being. Nor had she realized just how deep his ties to the community went. If she hadn't heard for herself, she'd have thought of Daniel Cobb solely as a ladies' man, but he was far more than the image he portrayed to the world.

After they'd smiled for several photographs with the starting lineup for the Miami Heat, Daniel took her to the Hyde lounge where they would have a bite before dinner.

The lavish supper club was the ultimate experience, and Angela luxuriated in the appeal of being waited on with private bottle service at the table. Daniel was sparing no expense, and she couldn't help wondering if he'd prearranged this for Alejandro Rivera. Or was this all for her?

She didn't know.

And she didn't care.

She was having too much fun seeing how the other half lived.

And Daniel was just the man to show her.

"You're just a mass of contradictions," Angela said when he regaled her with stories over appetizers and champagne. She hadn't objected when Daniel had requested a bottle of an expensive champagne. Instead, she sipped the delicious drink, allowing it to delight her taste buds.

"What do you mean?"

"You come off that you're all about business," Angela replied, "but there are many layers to you. Perhaps some you don't want to be seen."

"I'm showing them tonight, to you," Daniel responded, picking up his champagne flute and taking a sip. He held her gaze over the rim of the flute.

"Yes, you are," Angela said. "Joshua mentioned that Prescott George fund-raises for charity. What else do they do?"

Daniel filled her in on his volunteer efforts with the organization that supported black youth. "I participate when time permits and when I can't, I open my checkbook. But don't go giving me all the accolades. I'm not the only member of Prescott George who gives back to the community. Even though it's our mission statement, they're words we all live by."

"Very commendable," Angela said. "And when you're not giving back, what does Daniel Cobb do to relax?"

Over the remainder of the meal, they laughed and talked, and Angela found herself dropping the guard she normally kept around herself in Daniel's presence and enjoying the moment. He was her boss, after all, but tonight he was a man. A man she was attracted to. And if the gazes he gave her when he thought she wasn't looking were any indication, he was just as attracted to her.

Once again she looked at him from underneath her lashes. There was no denying the chemistry between them. The eye contact alone sent a current of electricity humming through her veins, tingling every nerve ending. When the meal finally concluded, she was happy to move. She'd been as jittery as a coiled spring. It didn't help when Daniel helped her from her seat and grasped her hand in his again.

Her heart raced and her stomach quivered in nervous anticipation.

"Relax," he whispered as he walked her back to the arena with the other basketball fans. "I don't bite."

Angela wasn't so sure about that.

She wasn't surprised when his hand met the small of her back as they walked to their floor seats and she felt a rush of heat. Nor that her breath hitched when Daniel's thigh brushed hers as they sat down. She'd come out tonight under the assumption that she was spending the night with her boss while he wooed a client. Instead, she'd found herself on what was essentially a date with Daniel.

She was thankful when the lights dimmed and music blared, disturbing her thoughts as the speaker announced the starting lineup for the Charlotte Hornets. There were lots of boos in the crowd, but the momentum changed and sparked to life when they announced the Miami Heat.

"These seats are great," Angela said when they sat back down after the national anthem. They were at center court, in front of all the action. If Alejandro had come, he would have been very pleased.

"Thanks, I'm glad you like them."

Angela glanced sideways at him. "And do you bring all your women out to expensive basketball games and private dining?" As soon as she said the words, Angela realized they belied her innermost thoughts and that she was curious about his love life.

"All my women?" Daniel snorted. He glanced behind his shoulder. "I don't see a gaggle of women lined up to date me."

"Oh, c'mon," Angela said, "don't be coy."

Daniel grinned broadly. "I get around."

"So you admit you're a player?"

"Who, me?" He shrugged. "Never. *My women*, as you call them, know the score. And so what if I treat them well? I don't make any illusions about my goals and objectives for the future."

The Heat scored a three-point basket and Daniel jumped out of his seat, clapping furiously. Angela liked this relaxed side of Daniel just as much as she liked seeing him in the jeans he wore. She was sure they were designer, as were the shirt and loafers he had on. Daniel exuded sophistication and class even when he dressed casually.

"Ahem!" Daniel coughed, returning her focus back to his face.

Angela blushed, and she could feel her cheeks stain red at having been caught checking him out. "Sorry."

"I don't mind when a beautiful woman stares at me like that."

"Daniel…"

"What?" he asked innocently. But she knew he knew better.

"You're flirting."

"And what's wrong with a little innocent flirting among friends?"

"Uh, I think it's more like employer-employee."

His eyes turned dark. "Not tonight."

Angela swallowed at the implication. Was he saying that what happened tonight wasn't on the record? So they could indulge in whatever fantasy their creative minds cooked up? If so, Angela was thinking of all sorts of things she'd love to do to Daniel, like ride him in the back of the limo while they drove the streets of Miami.

Where in the world had that come from?

She wasn't an exhibitionist and she liked to keep her private life private. However, there was a tiny part of her that had kicked into overdrive at the thought. From afar, she'd always found Daniel intriguing and sexy as hell, but in person with all his attention focused on her, he was so much more.

"Penny for your thoughts."

Angela chuckled. "I'd expected a lot more from you, Daniel. Like a five, maybe even twenty. I don't just let anyone into my head."

He threw back his head and laughed. "I like you, Angela. I like you a lot."

I like you a lot?

What had possessed him to verbalize what he'd been thinking? Angela. And those warm brown eyes of hers.

They'd beguiled him all night. As did her beauty. Those loose blond-streaked curls. Flawless skin. Sexy figure. It made him want her, *burn* for her. He wanted nothing more than to take her back to his place and fill her until she surrendered to the passion that had been simmering between them all night.

But he couldn't.

It wasn't right.

But that didn't stop him from wanting what he couldn't have.

The game was a nail-biter, with the Heat clinching the win in the last minute with a three-point shot and a foul. When it was over, they walked back toward where the limo had dropped them off earlier. Daniel pulled Angela closer to his side when the throng of people pushed her forward. That was the wrong move.

With Angela so near, Daniel could smell the sweet scent of her hair, catch a hint of the perfume she was wearing and feel her breasts pressed against his biceps.

Eventually the throng dissipated and Daniel was able to weave them through the crowd to the VIP area where the chauffeur stood waiting for them. He tipped his hat to them as he opened the door. Angela entered and Daniel was close behind her.

Once the door closed, the sexual tension between them was palpable and so thick it could be cut with a knife. Angela sat with her eyes downward and her hands folded in her lap. Daniel wanted to ruffle her feathers, make her feel as undone as he'd felt all night.

"Angela," he whispered her name.

She half turned in his direction, and that was all the invitation Daniel needed to act on his attraction.

* * *

Angela saw something akin to lust flash in Daniel's eyes just before he grasped both sides of her face and lowered his head. And when his lips brushed across hers in a kiss so slow and sensual, Angela felt her entire body come alive. But he didn't stop with one kiss. His mouth settled over hers, parting her lips with a lick of his tongue and giving her a jolt of excitement she hadn't felt in a long time, if ever.

He covered her body with his and then she felt his hands in her hair, holding her head still as he took her mouth like a thirsty man in search of his oasis. She returned the pressure of Daniel's kiss, instinctively moving her mouth over his as desire, hot and needy, coursed through her. Her heart hammered loudly in her chest, as did the knowledge that what they were doing was wrong. Her brain was telling her there was no way she should be doing this with Daniel. *Her boss.* Her brain told her to pull away. But her senses were seduced by his drugging kisses.

And when he deepened the kiss, she met him stroke for stroke, touching his tongue with hers, eager for the stimulation. The sensation was such sweet pleasure, she wanted to moan aloud, but she couldn't. He was nipping at her lower lip with his teeth while his hands were everywhere, palming her backside and then sliding upward to cup her breasts.

Angela shuddered when the pads of his thumbs caressed her nipples. She was sure they were protruding through the silk blouse, showing Daniel how turned on she was. She wanted his kisses to go on and on, but instead, he moved from her lips, bent his head and took one taut peak in his mouth. Angela thought she would combust in flames at the touch of his hot, wet tongue circling her nipple. He sucked her nipple, hard and deep, through her shirt. Daniel was making her feel more alive, wilder and hotter than she'd ever known was possible.

And when he adjusted their position, Angela ended up sprawled on the seat with Daniel hovering above her. Then he settled himself between her thighs, ensuring that the rock-hard steel of him was pressed against her center. Angela's mind went blank with need and she began to rock herself against him. Heat. Delight. She was experiencing so many emotions, so many sensations.

It was like she was caught up in a lightning storm. She wasn't sure if she would survive it—survive Daniel— and deep down some part of her didn't care if she did. She wanted this man, so much so that she shamelessly moved against him.

Daniel lifted his head from her breasts. "You're killing me, Angela," he growled, halting her hips with his hands.

"Why stop? If it's what we both want."

Daniel swore and slowly pulled away from Angela to sit upright, leaning his head back against the cushions. He took in a ragged breath. She was right. They both wanted it, the kiss and a whole lot more, because the pull had been that strong.

But Angela worked for him, and he'd just complicated the situation by acting first. He rubbed his face with both hands. "I'm sorry."

"Sorry?"

He glanced over and watched as she tried to finger-comb her hair and rearrange her clothes.

He'd done that.

He'd been the initiator.

He knew he was begging for trouble kissing her, but he couldn't help himself. And touching her? He'd finally been able to slide his hands up those sweet round hips of hers as he'd wanted to do all night long each time she'd strutted in front of him in those sexy red leather jeans.

He'd acted on his desire before, but since when had lust ever made him this way? This out of control? His body had actually trembled when he'd kissed her, and he felt dangerously close to taking her right there and then. He needed to get home and take an ice-cold shower until his erection subsided.

"Yes, I'm sorry," Daniel affirmed, taking in another gulp of air. "I should have never crossed the line."

"Well, you did," she responded. "*We* did. And now there's no going back. If we try, I think we'll both be miserable."

"So what do you suggest we do about it?"

Angela shrugged. "I dunno, maybe hang out a little bit. Perhaps it's just a onetime thing and it'll just fizzle out if we act on our desire."

Even as she said the words, Daniel knew she didn't believe them any more than he did. The attraction between them was hot, combustible, and the more time they spent in each other's company, the hotter it was going to be.

"I don't know how to do this," he said, pointing between the two of them, "and work together. Be your boss."

"It's one night. That's all that's on the table."

"I don't know," Daniel said. Angela wasn't one of his women who knew the score and would be content with being wined, dined, romanced and then set free. It could get complicated, messy. "I think it's best if we keep our relationship professional."

Angela nodded, but her eyes were cloudy and he couldn't read what she was thinking. "Of course, if that's what you prefer."

Darn it! It's not what he preferred. He would prefer to take Angela back to his place and ravish her body all night until they both were spent from pleasure. But theirs was an untenable situation. He didn't want to hurt Angela or cause damage to Cobb Luxury Real Estate in the process. He'd already done enough damage tonight by his impetuous actions.

"Good," he said. "I'm glad we've settled it."

They drove the remainder of the way to her apartment in awkward silence, and when the car came to a stop, Daniel started to get out, but Angela halted him. "Don't bother," she said curtly. "I can find my own way up."

Soon, she was exiting the vehicle with the help of the chauffeur and leaving Daniel sitting inside the limousine feeling like a complete and utter heel for having complicated the relationship and then cooled it off all in one night.

What the hell had he done?

Chapter 6

Angela awoke the next morning thankful that she didn't have to go into the office and face Daniel. After brushing her teeth and washing her face, she padded to the kitchen to make herself a cup of coffee, as if somehow it would wash away the memories of the night before and how she'd made a total fool out of herself.

She'd practically thrown herself at Daniel after he'd made the first move, but instead of taking her up on her offer of spending the night together, he'd told her no thanks. How humiliating! She didn't make a habit of throwing herself at wealthy, eligible bachelors. Sure, she liked the finer things in life and had appreciated all the effort Daniel had shown last night in wining and dining her, but she certainly should not have propositioned the man.

Whatever had gotten into her? Last night she'd had

a lapse in judgment. She'd gotten caught up in the moment, in the hype of being with Daniel Cobb, one of the Millionaire Moguls, and she'd made a play for him. And promptly fell flat on her face. Of course he wouldn't be interested in her—a junior real estate agent with hardly any money to speak of. The fact that she was saving up for what was probably a modest condo in Daniel's opinion was laughable.

He went out with highly successful, beautiful women. Though she wouldn't knock herself in the beauty department. She knew she wasn't bad on the eyes and that had always been her saving grace, but she also wanted respect. Maybe Daniel's brush-off was a way of showing respect? Showing that he valued their working relationship too much to ruin it?

But how on earth was she supposed to shadow him and let Daniel mentor her when there was this attraction simmering beneath the surface? Angela didn't know how she would fare, but apparently it was going to be pretty easy for Daniel. He'd made his feelings perfectly clear in the limo. He was interested in only one relationship with Angela and that was a professional one.

Later that afternoon, Angela was surprised when her sister Denise called and asked to meet her for coffee at a Cuban coffee shop near Coconut Grove. She'd known Denise was due back soon, but where had the time gone? She knew where she'd been—fantasizing about an affair with Daniel that would never happen.

After they placed their coffee orders and picked out their pastries, Angela and Denise found a two-seater table near the rear of the shop.

"It's so good to see you, sis," Angela said. "Though

I was surprised to hear from you. I thought you weren't making it back for another week."

"I wasn't," Denise responded, "but I decided to come back early because I wanted to talk to you about Mom and Dad's thirtieth anniversary party."

"I hadn't realized it was coming up so soon," Angela remarked as she took a pinch off the blueberry muffin she'd purchased.

Denise raised a brow. "Yes, well, I thought it would be nice, since they didn't celebrate their silver anniversary, that we throw them a party. You know, do something real nice."

"That sounds lovely," Angela responded. "But who is going to pay for this shindig?"

Denise shrugged. "I was hoping now that you're working at that big fancy real estate firm that you could. I mean, doesn't one of your commissions pay for an entire month's rent or something like that?" She chuckled nervously. "I do watch *Million Dollar Listing Miami*, and those guys make a killing."

"I'm sorry to tell you, little sis, that not all of us make those kinds of commissions," Angela returned. "I just joined Cobb six months ago and I'm far from getting clients like those you see on a television show."

Their coffee order was called by the barista and since Denise didn't lift a finger to get them, Angela rose from her chair and went for their drinks.

"So why keep up the front?" Denise asked when Angela returned and handed her the iced coffee she'd ordered. "Why don't you go back to school so you can get a real job?"

"I have a *real* job," Angela responded crisply. "In case you hadn't noticed, it's the one paying for this meal and that helps you out in grad school when you're in need of cash."

"Okay, okay." Denise held up her hands in defense. "I didn't mean to offend."

"What did you mean?" Angela replied. "Because on the one hand, you want me to pay for our parents' anniversary party, yet on the other, you're putting down how I make a living."

"I'm sorry, okay," Denise huffed. "Who knew you were so sensitive on the subject."

Angela sighed. Was she being too hard on her baby sister? She was just tired of everyone ragging on her job. Why couldn't they see that she could be quite successful at it?

Look at Daniel.

Thinking of her boss brought back the shame of last night and Angela flushed with embarrassment.

"Hey." Denise reached across the table and placed her hand over Angela's. "I'm sorry. Okay? Truly sorry that I offended you. You know I love you."

Angela blinked several times, bringing herself back to the present. "I know." She patted Denise's hand encouragingly.

"Is something else going on?"

Angela shook her head. She certainly wasn't about to spill her guts to her baby sister about an inappropriate relationship with her boss in a profession her family didn't fully support. "No, I'm just a little touchy on the subject of my career. I believe in what I'm doing, Denise, and all of you are going to have to get on board with that."

"I will," Denise replied. "Though you know Mom and Dad are academics, so it might be a little harder for them to come around, but you won't hold that against them, will you? You'll help with the party?"

Angela didn't hesitate to respond. "Of course I will, but we'll need to discuss budget. I'm working toward a goal, and I won't let anyone or anything get in the way of it."

"Thank you for making the time to meet with me," Joshua said when Daniel stopped by the yacht club where Joshua's private vessel was moored that afternoon. The yacht was exactly like its owner, sleek and sophisticated without trying too hard.

"It's no problem," Daniel responded.

"Care for a drink?" Joshua inquired.

"Scotch, neat."

While Joshua set about making his drink, Daniel gave him the once-over. From what he was wearing, no one would ever know Joshua was a member of the prestigious Prescott George, because he danced to the beat of his own drum. Even now, he wore cargo shorts and a cotton V-neck T-shirt that revealed a small tattoo of the infinity symbol on his right biceps. The only reason anyone would know he had any money was his Ray-Ban aviator sunglasses and Jack & Jones leather boat shoes.

Daniel didn't mind. Nor did it bother him that everything came easy to Joshua. Or so it seemed to Daniel. As a corporate raider, Joshua appeared to make his fortune from the misfortune of others, but his natural charisma made everyone he came into contact with a believer, all except Ashton. Daniel suspected the club president was the real reason Joshua wanted to meet privately on his yacht, and away from public eyes and ears. Although the paparazzi had a passing fascination with Daniel because he used social media as a means to an end for his business, they *loved* Joshua, because he catered to them.

"Why all the cloak-and-dagger?" Daniel teased when Joshua walked over and handed him his scotch.

"I think you know why," Joshua said, sitting across from him. "It's time we oust Ashton."

"Cutting to the chase. I appreciate your directness."

"And?" Joshua leaned forward, bracing his elbows on his thighs. "Are you on board with helping me on this? You've been a member of PG a helluva lot longer than me. People respect you, listen to you."

"Yeah, well, I'm sure with your charisma, you can bring the other members around."

"Not without your support." Joshua swigged his beer and leaned back in his chair. "You've known Ashton a long time and everyone knows it. If you say our practices are outdated, folks will listen."

"It won't be easy dethroning Ashton," Daniel said. "There's never been a time in the organization's history when a Rollins or an Owens hasn't been in command. There's a legacy there, Joshua. You would do well to remember that."

"Yeah, well, it's time for a change," Joshua responded. "Ashton is still clinging to some twentieth-century way of doing things. It's the twenty-first century, Daniel. You and I know that the only way we'll keep Prescott George moving upward is to recognize that."

"I agree with you."

"But are you *with* me?" Joshua asked. "Ready to do battle with me, against Ashton? I know it won't be easy. He recommended you for the club. It'll feel like a betrayal if you turn on him."

"Then he would know how it feels," Daniel murmured under his breath.

"What was that?"

"Nothing." Daniel rose from the lounger, downed the rest of his scotch and turned to face his friend. "I'm in."

A broad grin spread across Joshua's mouth. "That's good to hear." He stood to shake Daniel's hand. "You won't regret this."

Daniel snorted. "I'm sure I will, but there's no turning back." He started toward the plank that led to the marina.

"Daniel, if you don't mind my asking," Joshua started, "there seems to be some sort of bad blood between you and Ashton. Care to share? Because in my quest to bring Ashton down, I'm not going to leave any stone unturned. If you have news that might be helpful…"

"None I'd care to share," Daniel responded evenly. "We'll talk soon."

Daniel moved down the plank and toward his Ferrari. He was in no mood for personal confessions. He wasn't about to share with anyone, let alone Joshua, his unrequited love for Mia and how she'd chosen Ashton over him. That was his cross to bear and his alone.

Chapter 7

Monday morning arrived and Angela was determined to put the past seventy-two hours behind her. So what if she'd made out with her boss like some kind of wanton woman who was hard up to get laid. Daniel had rebuffed her. Made her feel as insignificant as the women they talked about in the press.

But Angela wouldn't let his rejection ruin her career. She had a good thing going at Cobb Luxury Real Estate, and if she kept her cool, her reputation would only grow. One day she'd have her own million-dollar listings instead of following Daniel around.

To her good fortune, she didn't see Casanova much over the next two days. Every time she came in, he was either not in the office or on his way out. That was just fine with Angela. She didn't relish having to work so closely with the man. Not after she'd found him immensely attractive while he'd remained cool and aloof, despite the swell in his pants that she'd felt.

How did he manage it? Had his heart not pounded at their electrifying kiss? Clearly, it hadn't been as momentous as it had been for her.

It wasn't until midafternoon on Wednesday that Daniel decided to face her. Or should she say, he had Myrna call her into his office.

Angela took a huge fortifying breath as she walked ramrod straight toward his office. She was glad that today she was looking her best in a bright orange sheath that showed off her hourglass shape, peep-toe stilettos, and colorful bangles and earrings. Angela had to admit she looked sharp.

When she reached his door, she waited for an invite and he waved her forward.

"You asked to see me?" she inquired from the doorway. She'd come prepared with her folio to take notes.

Daniel lifted his gaze from his monitor and looked straight at her. His mouth settled on her bare shoulders, then his eyes traveled down the length of her. The air throbbed with tension, and Angela could feel heat spreading through her body as it instantly responded to him.

She swallowed it back. Her face blazed, but instead of lowering her lashes at his blatant perusal, she stared back boldly at him. "Daniel?"

He blinked several times as if he was bringing her into focus. "Yes?"

"If now isn't a good time, I can come back."

"No, no, now is fine. Please sit." He gestured to the seat in front of him and then rose from his chair to close the door she'd purposely left open. "I wanted to talk to you about ideas for the launch of the Wilsons' estate."

Angela took a seat in one of the two chairs. "I have a few ideas."

"Let's hear them." Daniel sat on the edge of his glass desk. He was so close, their legs almost touched. Angela crossed her legs to give them distance and she noted that Daniel caught the action, but didn't say anything.

She opened her folio. "Well, as you mentioned, we could have a talented musician come in and play for the crowd. You know, to get them excited. Or I thought we could have an art showing, displaying several pieces of artwork from local artists."

"Go on."

"Or we could go a little unconventional and play up the exclusivity of Sunny Isles with our social media."

"Hmm…" Daniel rubbed his jaw. "Sounds very promising."

"Which one?"

"I like the last one."

"You do?" Angela knew it was a risky move, but the buzz they could gain might make buyers come to the opening.

"Yes," Daniel said. "We need traffic, and to get the word out about the property."

Angela beamed with pride. She couldn't believe Daniel really thought her idea was worthwhile.

"I'd like you to run lead on it," Daniel continued. "I'll send you the vCard for my marketing firm. They're the only folks I trust to provide marketing materials for my high-profile clients." He reached behind him for his iPad, and with several swipes of his finger he was done and set it back down on the desk.

"Thank you. I appreciate your faith in me." Angela

rose to leave, but Daniel stopped her by placing his hand on her waist.

"Did I say the meeting was over?"

Angela glanced down at his hand, which he immediately moved. "Uh, no." She sat back down in her chair. "Was there something else?"

"Yes, I wanted to go tour the model condo of our new development downtown. It's finally ready and I thought you might want to join me."

"Do you really think that's a good idea?"

"I am your mentor, am I not?"

"Yes, I just…" Her words trailed off. If Daniel could act as if this past weekend had never happened, so could she. "I'll get my purse."

Daniel watched Angela out the corner of his eye as she walked through the model, which had been decorated by one of the top home stagers in the business.

Instead of assessing the property, he was too busy studying her.

He admired her long, straight brown hair highlighted with blond streaks and the proud tilt of her head. She was putting up a good front that she was unaffected by him, and he admired her determination. She was refusing to allow what had occurred between them to deter her career. While he, on the other hand, was having a hard time not remembering how good it had felt to hold her. How good it had felt to have the soft press of her breasts against his chest. How good she'd tasted when they'd kissed.

He'd tried pushing thoughts of her from his mind, but there was no escaping her. She was at his office. They were showing property together. He was just going to have to face what was going on between them…but how?

He didn't do relationships. Never had. The memory of Mia and her rejection had been seared in his memory. He never wanted to give his love so freely without knowing if it was returned. And after a time, he'd decided that he didn't need love. If he dated a woman for too long and she became clingy, he ended it. Since Mia there really hadn't been another woman to keep his attention or interest for long, in or out of bed, except one. His ex, Farrah Davenport. She'd traded on her beauty for tangible items and the extravagant gifts he could provide her, hoping to string him along until her inevitable endgame: marriage. Not that her plays had worked. He'd called it quits with her.

But Angela intrigued him. She didn't appear to be like any other woman he'd known, making him want to delve deeper, beyond what was on the surface.

But he squashed any hopes she'd had the other night in the limo when he'd made it clear that theirs was a *business* relationship. So why was he still yearning for this woman? And not just her body. He wanted to know what motivated her, what drove her. What she liked. What— Well, he wanted to know everything about her.

She turned to face him and her eyes were lit up. "This place is pretty amazing, wouldn't you agree?"

"It's certainly going to raise the bar downtown."

"Which is pretty hard considering the many developments under way," Angela responded. "So how do we set this apart?"

"One of the keys to success is looking at each project individually and giving your singular focus to it in that moment. If you don't believe wholeheartedly in the product you're selling, why should the buyer?"

"Even if it's up to fifteen hundred dollars per square foot?" Angela inquired. The price point the developer set for Daniel to achieve was staggering, and he expected Daniel to sell 25 percent of the project at the launch party.

"Even then," Daniel said. "We'll reach out to all my contacts. Make the event the place to be seen. Generate lots of buzz on social media. We need to be talking about it to every potential buyer. Tell them it's synonymous with luxury. Sell them on the dream."

Angela stared back at him.

"What?"

"You're selling me," Angela said, "and I can't afford to buy even the one-bedroom in this place."

"You will one day." Daniel walked to the French doors and opened them to show off the view of the Atlantic Ocean.

"From your lips to God's ears," she responded, coming out to join him. "This is a quite a view and with the sun setting..." Her voice trailed off.

Daniel observed Angela. As she closed her eyes and soaked in the ambience, he wanted to kiss her. Right then and there. She looked so soft and appealing with her hair gently tousled by the wind that he wanted to take her in his arms and remind himself exactly how good it felt to have her there.

Would she fight him if he kissed her? Push him away as he'd done her?

He stepped toward her, his mouth just inches away from hers. As if she felt his warmth, her eyes flickered open. Stopping short a few inches away from her, he settled his gaze on the seductive curve of her lips. His heart began thundering loudly in his chest and his groin tightened as lust ripped through him. He had to make a hasty retreat, so she wouldn't see the evidence of just how turned on he was. "Ready to go?" He spun on his heel quickly and headed toward the French doors.

"Yes," she said softly and followed behind him.

Once he was alone in the car, since they'd driven separately, Daniel's senses were reeling. If only she'd kept her eyes closed a moment longer, he would have known just how close to heaven he'd truly been because he'd have kissed her.

But she had opened her eyes and now he was going to have to go home and take a very long shower to wash away the hunger he had for Angela.

Chapter 8

After the near kiss with Daniel, Angela did her best to stay busy. If she hadn't opened her eyes on the balcony, she was certain he would have kissed her. She was a woman, after all, and knew when a man was attracted to her. And she hadn't imagined the pure, unadulterated lust that had been in his eyes.

He'd wanted her.

But instead of acting on it, he'd walked away, leaving them both bereft and frustrated. Angela didn't make a habit out of workplace romances, but in this instance she was willing to concede the point. She'd been so focused on her rising real estate career that she hadn't left much room in her life for romance.

She'd been celibate for two years, and she'd felt every minute of it with Daniel. It had been too long since she'd been kissed. Touched. Held in a man's arms. Was her desire for Daniel just some latent reaction to being alone or was there more to it? She was afraid to look too closely.

She returned from two afternoon showings for a mid-level condo on Thursday afternoon. When she made it back to the office, it was just past 5:00 p.m., Myrna was clearing her desk for the day and most of the sales associates were departing.

"What are you doing back here today?" Myrna inquired.

"Busy afternoon. And I promised some sales comps to my clients tomorrow, so I thought I'd come in and get it wrapped up."

"All right," Myrna said, "but don't stay too late."

"I won't. See you in the morning." As Angela walked back to her desk, she caught sight of Daniel sitting in his office huddled over his computer. Apparently, she wasn't the only one working late. If he didn't see her, she could knock out those comps and be done before he was the wiser.

Angela headed straight for her office and began working. She'd been going at a steady pace for nearly two hours when she sensed his presence at her doorway. Daniel had a barely leashed energy that vibrated off him and made everyone take notice. A disturbing heat stirred in her belly.

Glancing up from her monitor, Angela saw Daniel and her heart jolted. She straightened her back, desperate not to show any sign of weakness. "Mr. Cobb."

He grimaced. "You don't have to call me Mr. Cobb. Daniel will do."

"Are you sure about that?" she asked and returned to the keyboard to finish typing the email she'd been preparing. "Because I wouldn't want to cross any boundaries."

"Angela…"

"Yes?" She swiveled around in her executive chair.

Daniel seemed as if he wanted to say something else. Maybe apologize for how he'd behaved the other night, sending her away as if he hadn't initiated that kiss that had sent both of them spiraling out of control? Instead, he said, "I thought we could sit and talk. I've ordered up some sushi from a great take-out place. We can eat in the conference room."

The last thing Angela wanted was to be alone with Daniel, and as she glanced up and peered through the glass panels of her office, it appeared they were the only souls left on the floor. "I can't."

"Of course you can," he replied. "You have to eat. C'mon." He inclined his head toward the door.

Angela was torn. Did she obey an order from her boss? Or should she listen to her female intuition, which told her it was dangerous to be alone with Daniel?

She chose to follow his directive and rose from her chair, smoothing down her dress as she went.

When she walked into the conference room, Angela discovered the sushi had already arrived and was sitting in several plastic containers along with bowls of soup. Had Daniel set this up? Was this some sort of peace offering?

"Sit."

Angela did as instructed and Daniel did the same, sitting across from her. He reached for a plastic container. "I hope you like sushi, because I got a little bit of everything."

"I love it." Angela smiled and reached for a container. Inside she discovered a mix of California, spicy tuna and Bubba rolls. Daniel slid a pair of chopsticks her way with a questioning brow.

"I can use them," Angela responded, and deftly removed them from the wrapper and picked up a roll. She plopped it in her mouth with ease and moaned at the delicious taste.

Daniel felt his shaft spring to life at the tiny moan that escaped from Angela's pink-tinted lips. It reminded him of how she'd sounded when she'd been underneath him in that limo. When they'd kissed so passionately.

How could he forget it? He'd been able to think of nothing since. And it was why tonight, against his better judgment, he'd stayed behind to work late. He'd seen Angela walk in just after five o'clock when he'd been nearly done with the project he was working on. But instead of going home as would have been wise, he'd stayed behind. Fooling about on work that could have waited until tomorrow.

Why? Because he'd wanted to spend time with her. Alone.

So he'd waited a sufficient amount of time to make it appear as if he'd been working just as hard and could casually ask her to eat dinner with him.

Angela, however, was focusing a lot of her attention on her food instead of conversing with him. He wanted to draw her out of her shell again, so he tried to engage her. "You're very good with those," he said, inclining his head in the direction of her chopsticks.

"Comes with practice. I spent some time in Asia as well as Europe after I ditched college after a year."

Daniel relaxed; their dinner was shifting and he could see her softening toward him as she had before. "Oh yeah? Where'd you go?"

"Tokyo, Singapore, Beijing," Angela said. "I wanted to see the world. Experience new cultures."

"Your parents couldn't have been happy with that decision."

She nodded. "They weren't. They were always upset that I left college and didn't return, but not everyone's meant for school. I wanted to see the world."

"And did you?"

She glanced up from her plate and looked over at him. "Hell yeah. Those years were some of the best I've ever had, even when I was basically broke half the time and working the odd job here and there to go to my next destination."

"Which was your favorite?"

"I really loved Thailand," Angela said. "The people were just so friendly and the food was the best of my travels, bar none."

"Even France? Or Italy?"

Angela nodded. "Although I loved Paris, Monte Carlo and the Italian coast, Thailand had the best food and the most spectacular views of the ocean."

"Your passport must be stamped full."

Angela shrugged. "I actually went through a couple during that period, but eventually I got homesick and wanted to put down roots. The problem was when I got back everyone I knew was in a different phase in their life and I kind of fell behind. Had to figure out my way."

"From where I'm sitting you have."

"Not like you," Angela responded. "You have a knack for salesmanship. Look at what you've accomplished."

"I watched my father and emulated him. He owned a small real estate firm and he made a decent living, but he never took it a step further. I saw potential there, a niche market that wasn't being tapped or catered to. He introduced me to some folks he knew and I took the ball and ran with it."

Angela laughed. "Why are you giving me the condensed version? Can't you be real with me?"

Daniel stared at her. "I am being real with you."

"Nope," she said as she shook her head. "You've told me the same thing I could read about you on the internet while I, on the other hand, have kept it one hundred with you."

He grinned at her slang. "No one wants to hear about my struggles to start a new firm in Miami."

"Try me."

"Are you always this pushy?"

Her brown eyes flashed fire. "It's got me this far in life. Why should I stop now?"

"All right." He let out a long sigh. "If you must know, I had to take out a small business loan, but it wasn't enough to cover the start-up costs for Cobb Luxury Real Estate."

"And?" She urged him to continue.

"The father of an associate of mine lent me the money." Daniel's mind went to Alexander Rollins and how he wouldn't be happy that Daniel was going against his son at Prescott George and supporting Joshua. But it wasn't like Alexander hadn't made a killing off the short-term investment and high interest. Daniel had paid him back. "In the end, I was able to open a small office. At first it was just me and Mary. She was my receptionist, my office manager and my marketing person all rolled into one, but I couldn't have started this place without her."

"Everyone loves Mary."

"As they should. She's been like a mother to me."

"And what of your own mom? Where is she?"

Daniel shrugged. "She lives in Tampa. Remarried after she caught my father cheating. Started a new life with a new family. Don't see her much." He didn't want to think about those dark days when he'd felt abandoned. Instead, he wanted their conversation to be upbeat. "Was that real enough for you, Angela? Am I keeping it one hundred enough now?"

She stared at him for several long moments before speaking. "It was." Then she laughed. "But don't start speaking slang. Doesn't really suit you." She rose from her chair and leaned over to gather the plastic containers on the table.

"I can help." Daniel stood and they both reached for a container at the same time. Their eyes locked from across the table. Daniel didn't let go of the container and neither did Angela. Instead, an invisible force pulled them closer and closer to each other.

When they were mere inches apart and Daniel could breathe in the fruity notes of her perfume, he thought about whether this was the right decision. He knew he should banish all thoughts of Angela from his mind, but he'd been going crazy for days trying to ignore her. Acting as if he didn't notice her in the office.

He just had to touch her. He reached out and caressed her cheek with his palm.

"Don't." Angela tried to turn away, but he slowly pulled her back toward him.

"Angela." The precarious control he'd been holding on to finally snapped and his nostrils flared. She looked like she was ready for his mouth on hers. And without thinking of the consequences or whether it was right or wrong, he wrapped one arm around her hips and pulled her close to him, then he kissed her.

He kissed her like a starving man, again and again. Threading his fingers through her hair, he plundered her lips like he'd never kissed a woman's before. At first her palms were flat against his chest, but within seconds she wrapped them around his neck and was matching him stroke for stroke. Daniel leaned her over the table and took his fill. He'd fantasized about kissing Angela again, and he couldn't fight his desire any longer. The pull was too great.

So he gave in.

Angela yielded to the kiss. She now knew what she'd known in that limo: Daniel was as into her as she was him. He was just better at hiding it, until now. She knew being with Daniel spelled danger, but her body was responding to his as if they fit together like two perfect puzzle pieces. His lips grazed over hers, using the right amount of pressure to coax a low moan from her.

The opening gave Daniel the entry he sought and his tongue darted inside, flicking against hers. Angela eagerly gave him the friction they both needed, mating her tongue with his and basking in the wild sensations he evoked. She surrendered herself to it because Daniel was bringing alive a vibrancy in her, an intensity of feeling she'd never had.

Daniel was staking a claim and burning a need in her at the same time. When he tore his mouth from hers, it was a dizzying shock to her senses and she pressed her head against his shoulder, clutching him. But instead of stopping, he placed openmouthed kisses on her neck while his hands traveled down her hips and thighs.

Angela wanted more. So she didn't stop him when he lifted the hem of her dress. His hands were hot and warm as they traveled over her, kneading her fevered flesh along the way. As much as she reveled in the feel of his hands, she burned for him to touch her in that one special place.

The closer his hands inched toward her core, the more her insides began to quake, and when he finally pushed the silky fabric of her panties aside and eased one finger inside her, Angela moaned aloud.

"Daniel…" He slid in another finger and her breath caught in her throat. His fingers began slow and gentle thrusts in and out. Angela arched her hips, her head flying backward.

"Don't stop," she said when he removed his fingers, scooped her up and placed her on the conference room table. The next thing she knew, he was sliding her dress all the way up to her waist. When he pressed her legs apart and to her shock knelt on the floor and lowered his head to her, Angela couldn't believe what was happening. She didn't have time to, because Daniel caught her with his mouth.

She screamed as he sucked her, his tongue dancing up and down the bundle of nerves at her core. It had been too long since she'd been with a man, too long since she'd felt this good. So it didn't take long for her orgasm to start building. Shamelessly, she pumped against his mouth, and he grasped her bottom in his hands and tongued her feverishly.

Pressure built inside her until it erupted. Wave after wave of pleasure hit her in full force and she bucked and moaned on the table. Daniel held her legs, lapping up her juices as Angela tried to breathe normally.

But it was impossible; her heart was thumping so loud in her chest, she was sure he could hear it. Daniel rose to his feet and bent over her, kissing her mouth. She could taste herself on his lips.

"I…" She didn't know where to begin and apparently,

neither did he, because he placed his finger on her lips and shook his head. How could he not want to talk about what had just happened? She'd just let her boss go down on her in the conference room.

Flushed with embarrassment, Angela slid off the table, lowered her dress and smoothed her hair, trying to pull herself together. She watched Daniel rub his temples and start pacing the floor. He was just as disoriented and shocked by what he'd allowed to happen as she was.

When he finally stopped, he turned to her. "I—I should walk you out."

"What?"

"I should walk you to your car. It's late."

"So that's it? You don't have anything else to say?"

Daniel sucked in a deep breath. "I—I think it's best we talk tomorrow when clearer heads prevail."

Angela stared in him in stunned disbelief. Was he really going to act like they just hadn't shared an incredibly intimate moment and could talk tomorrow?

"Don't bother, Daniel. I'm perfectly capable of looking after myself. I've done pretty well thus far, no thanks to you."

She turned and quickly stalked out of the room. She wasn't going to stand there and act like nothing happened. She wasn't Daniel's plaything that he could use to get his jollies off and discard whenever it suited him. *You were the one who orgasmed*, her inner voice reminded her, but she dismissed it.

He'd enjoyed the experience; she was positive of it. He'd better have gotten his fill, because it was the last time she was allowing Daniel to come near her ever again.

Chapter 9

As he stood under the rainfall shower in his penthouse condo later that night, Daniel was ashamed of how far he'd allowed the evening to go. He'd intended one kiss to ease the sexual tension simmering between them. Instead, he'd found nirvana between Angela's thighs.

He hadn't planned for it to go that far, but he'd found it irresistible the way she'd moaned and writhed underneath him when they kissed. He'd known she was hot for him, wet for him. And she had been. He'd felt it, tasted her sweet nectar.

Glancing down, Daniel was still hard. Hard for Angela. And thanks to his thoughtless behavior, he'd probably never get near her again. He'd been just as shocked as she'd been by the turn of events, but instead of facing it, he'd tried to sweep it under the rug, which angered Angela.

The shocked look on her face when he'd offered to walk her to her car had said it all. She was over the cat-and-mouse game between them, and it would take a miracle for him to ever get that close to her again.

Damn! He'd screwed that up royally.

Why was it so hard for him to tell her how he truly felt? Which was that he found her not only attractive, but vibrant and intelligent. Instead, he'd acted like a bumbling idiot and a far cry from the player the media made him out to be.

Tonight, they'd initially discussed superficial subjects, but eventually she'd opened up to him, sharing her past with him, and he was starting to see that she could become so much more than the unemotional entanglements he'd had previously. Used to seeing avarice in women's eyes, he'd become jaded thinking they all wanted only his wealth and material things. But Angela seemed just as content to share sushi with him at the office as she was in a VIP supper club.

Angela sat curled up on her couch with a glass of red wine. She'd opened a bottle after she showered, eager for the relaxation that a nightcap would bring.

The night had gotten out of control and she had no one to blame but herself. Yet again, she'd allowed the chemistry she shared with Daniel to negate her good sense. She knew better than to engage in an office romance with her mentor, her boss. But when he'd looked at her with eyes full of lust and when those full lips of his had touched her mouth, reason had gone out the window. Instead she'd indulged in the slowest, most sensual kiss from his wet lips and soft tongue.

No man had ever had this kind of effect on her. She'd

been with other men, had been intimate with them, but Daniel disarmed her. Every time she was around him she lost her senses. It was disconcerting.

Now she was left with regret.

Where did they go from here? How did she fix this? Denying they had an attraction for each other had ended with her skirt around her waist and Daniel's head between her legs.

Christ! She ran her fingers through her hair. This was a disaster of epic proportion. She didn't want to lose her job or leave Cobb Luxury Real Estate. It finally felt like she'd found her place and was on the right path for her career. Only to stumble when faced with Daniel Cobb.

What was she going to do?

The next morning she got up like she always did and put on a stunning white pantsuit with her four-inch heels. Angela needed to feel confident because she wasn't sure what she was facing at the office.

"Good morning," she called as she walked into the office, affecting confidence.

"Wow! Someone is dressed to impress," Myrna said as Angela swept past her. "Big meeting today? Do you need any help?"

"No, I've got it, Myrna. I stayed behind last night working on those comps so I would be ready, but thank you."

"Sure thing," Myrna responded. "I think someone else might be interested in seeing you, as well."

"Pardon me?"

Myrna inclined her head and Angela followed her gaze to find Daniel standing in the doorway of his office with a mug of coffee in his hands.

"Angela, a word?"

Angela sucked in a breath. Did they have to do this now? She hadn't even had her morning cup of joe. She'd been running late this morning after two glasses of wine last night.

She started on unsteady legs toward Daniel. "Yes?" she asked him, standing in the hallway so they were in public view of everyone in the office.

"I have several showings on the calendar today, so other than your morning meeting, you'll be spending most of your day with me. We also have dinner with Alejandro Rivera at the Forge tonight."

Angela didn't appreciate Daniel's high-handedness. He was forcing her to be alone with him and confront what happened between them last night when she'd rather hide out in her office. And did he have to do it looking so darn good in a crisp white shirt, skinny tie and gray slim-fit trousers?

She wanted to rail at him to give her some breathing room, but instead she measured her response and said, "You must have quite the pull. I've heard it's hard to get a last-minute reservation there."

"Not for me."

Angela nodded. "Very well. What time shall I meet you for the showing and where?"

"I thought we could drive together."

"I'd rather not."

She could see the wheels of his mind turning at her insubordination. "All right." He gave her the location and time to meet and then closed the door of his office behind him, leaving Angela wondering exactly what the hell Daniel was up to.

Annoyed, she rushed to her office so she could fume

in private. Didn't he realize that the more time they spent together, the harder it would be to resist the attraction between them? Or maybe that's exactly what he wanted, but was too afraid to act on it? Did Daniel expect her to chase *him*?

Angela was used to the shoe being on the other foot, but maybe she'd misjudged the situation. Maybe Daniel wanted her to take matters in her own hands and show him she had no reservations about taking their relationship to the next level?

But she'd already done that when she'd suggested they spend one night together. What more did he want?

Daniel used the smart device to turn on the lights, open the motorized blinds of the twelve-foot windows and flood the two-thousand-square-foot condo he was showing that morning with light. His assistant, Mary, had already ensured that Evian water and snacks had been laid out on the granite counter prior to his arrival. And he'd come early. Not just to make sure the listing was ready for showing, but to give himself time to prepare to spend the day with Angela. Last night, he'd resolved that he couldn't ignore her. If their conference room scene was any indication, that hadn't worked. He had to face his attraction to Angela head-on.

He'd hoped to talk to her in the car ride over. Perhaps suggest they go out for a meal and talk things over. He knew he was begging for trouble, but he couldn't help himself. Angela, however, didn't even want to be in the same car with him and had insisted on driving herself.

This morning, she'd stood outside his office in that sleek white suit looking stiff yet sexy as hell. His hands had ached to palm the shape of her bottom as he'd done last night when he'd hauled her against him, but she looked ready to bolt if he took two steps toward her.

It had been hard keeping his distance, so he'd stayed in the doorway, not forcing the issue. She had nothing to be embarrassed over. He'd been the aggressor. Kissing her like that. Hiking her skirt over her slender hips and having his way with her.

Daniel cursed silently. Why couldn't he stop thinking about her? He wasn't used to feeling any sort of emotion where women were concerned, especially after Mia. He was used to having them for one purpose—as a lover. He had no use for love or relationships. But Angela had him rethinking his position.

Not on love.

On whether he could sustain a relationship even in the short term. Perhaps if he just got this attraction out of his system, life could go back to normal. Yes, that was it. If they had sex, he could finally stop staying awake at night wondering what it would be like to have her underneath him.

The doorbell rang and he didn't need to answer it to know who it was. He sensed her.

Daniel strode over to the door and swung it open.

Angela was on the other side, just as he'd known she would be. "I'm sorry I'm late," she said, sweeping into the penthouse. "The Herreras were quite talkative this morning, and I kept looking at my watch hoping I would not be late."

"You can relax. You're still early and no one's shown up yet." He closed the door behind her. "I was just setting up."

"Need any help?" Angela removed the white jacket that matched the pants and hung it over the bar stool, revealing an expanse of bare back to Daniel's gaze. She spun around to face him and Daniel's eyes raked boldly over her. He lingered on the thin camisole she wore and the outline of her nipples thanks to the chill in the air.

"No, I've got it."

He watched her visibly shudder and then she reached for the jacket and quickly slid her arms back inside. Was she cold or had she guessed the lascivious thoughts running through his head?

"Great!" She turned her back to him and fiddled with her folio. "How many prospects are we expecting?"

"Four buyers and any number of brokers," Daniel said. "I've been talking this place up quite a bit to the top folks in town. I'm hoping to get an offer."

She spun around to face him. "That's pretty ambitious. Do you think that's possible?"

"I've been known to make the impossible happen," he stated emphatically. "The key is for them to see you as the authority in luxury real estate and the best in town."

"Good to know." She smiled at his bravado, and he was about to expand on the thought when the doorbell rang.

The afternoon was an endless parade of brokers stopping by to visit the penthouse. He made sure to introduce Angela to each one, and she followed him around observing how he handled them as well as the buyers, their questions and concerns. By the time the fourth buyer, a couple, came late in the afternoon, Daniel allowed Angela to tour them herself as he observed from a close distance.

She was a natural. She had an ease with the buyer that not only made them feel at home, but told them she was knowledgeable about the marketplace.

As she walked with the buyer and pointed out the features of the master bath and massive closet, their broker, Arthur Andersen, stood back with Daniel in the master bedroom. "You've got quite a talent there, Cobb," Arthur said.

Daniel eyed Angela. "Don't I know it."

"If you're not careful, one of the big boys might come and snatch her up."

His eyes narrowed as he stared at his colleague. "I wouldn't let that happen."

"Whoa! Don't get your briefs in a twist there, Cobb. I'm just pointing out that you can't hold good talent back. In time she'll want to spread her wings."

Daniel didn't intend to let that happen. Angela was his find. He'd known from the moment he'd met her at an open house for a competing broker that she had the chops to be successful. She just needed a little honing. And he'd love to hone every inch of that delectable body of hers.

"So what's up with you Millionaire Moguls?" Arthur inquired, breaking into his errant thoughts. "I heard there was some dissension among the ranks and there was some commotion at your monthly dinner."

"You shouldn't listen to gossip."

"I heard it from a reliable source. Anyway, you guys think you rule this town."

"That's because we do," Daniel responded. Arthur was not his friend. He was cordial to the man because convention required him to be, but he wouldn't trust the man as far as he could throw him.

"Glad to see you're just as arrogant as you've always been."

His clients and Angela exited the master bath and walk-in closet. She glanced at Daniel as if sensing friction between the two men. "How about this view?" She gave Daniel a wink and led the couple through to the adjoining balcony that overlooked Brickell Bay.

Several minutes later, after several oohs and aahs, they made their way to the lower level where the couple gushed about how much they loved the place. After Angela had poured them both another glass of champagne, she joined Daniel in the discussion.

"What's the ask?" Arthur asked.

"Full ask. Five million." He noticed that Angela didn't bat an eye even though he'd told her earlier that he was willing to concede by half a mil, but this guy irked Daniel. Always had, so he was in no mood to work with him on price.

"C'mon, Daniel," Arthur said. "My clients want to know they're getting a deal here."

"This is a deal. Every condo in the building has gone for upward of four million. And this is the penthouse. You've got to know that it's a higher price point especially with the vaulted ceilings areas on the lower level."

"And the balcony off the master suite." Angela joined. "Have you seen anything like it? You can't beat the views."

"You're reaching, Daniel, but then why am I not surprised." Arthur snorted. "And now you have your girl Friday here, following after you like a good lapdog."

Angela opened her mouth to speak, but Daniel touched her arm and shook his head.

"Let me talk it over with my clients," Arthur said.

Once he'd stepped away, Angela seethed with fury by Daniel's side. "The gall of that man to call me a lapdog!"

"Ignore him. I do. He isn't worth your anger."

"Are all the top brokers in town like him?" she whispered.

"Some," Daniel answered honestly, "but because of it, his client will pay through the nose."

Arthur returned several minutes later. "My clients are willing to offer full ask."

A broad grin spread across Daniel's lips and he gave Angela a knowing look. They'd done it. They'd sold the penthouse together. They were a good team.

And, Daniel suspected, they'd be even better lovers. But would he have another chance to convince her of that?

Chapter 10

Angela couldn't help but admire Daniel even though he wore a smug smile as he sat in the bar at the Forge, where they were dining with Alejandro Rivera. She'd had just enough time after their showings to go home, shower and change before Daniel's limo arrived to pick her up.

But this time, its owner was not in it. Had he known that sitting together in close quarters again was a recipe for disaster? She hadn't minded the bottle of Cristal that had been left chilling for her and helped herself to some on the ride over. She could get very used to this extravagant lifestyle.

Tonight, she'd chosen a simple black midi dress with cutaway armholes. It was feminine yet sleek, and showed off her curves and a fair amount of her back with the crisscross detail. It wasn't designer but from a fashionable boutique in town. She'd piled her hair in a loose updo with tendrils of curls framing her face.

Daniel was obviously pleased with the outfit. He showed his appreciation by raking her with a searing gaze.

"Is Alejandro not here?" Angela inquired once she'd sat in one of the bar stools beside Daniel. He was nursing a scotch while she'd ordered a martini. "I'd have thought he'd be here by now." She'd purposely arrived fifteen minutes late, not wanting to be alone with Daniel.

He shook his head, but his eyes never left her face. "He called to say he'd hit some traffic but he'll be here any minute. Speaking of…here he is now."

Angela spun around to face the six-foot Colombian with thick dark hair, a chiseled jaw with a goatee, and dark eyes. He wore an expensive Italian suit and loafers. "Daniel, it's good to see you, my friend, but who is this lovely creature next to you?"

Daniel turned to Angela. "Alejandro, this is Angela Trainor. She's an associate in my firm whom I'm mentoring. Angela, this is Alejandro Rivera."

Angela extended her hand. "It's a pleasure to meet you."

Alejandro grasped her hand in his. He held it for a minute longer than was conventional before brushing his lips across the top. Angela smiled, but quickly withdrew her hand.

"She is lovely, Daniel," he said. "I can't wait to spend more time with you this evening." He held out his arm.

Angela didn't want to accept it. The kiss on her hand a moment ago had been a little forward, but she didn't want to offend one of Daniel's biggest potential clients, so she accepted his proffered arm. He clasped his hand over hers.

"Are you ready to be seated, Mr. Cobb?" the host inquired.

"Yes, we are."

"Allow me to show you to your room."

Alejandro walked with Angela, leaving Daniel to follow behind them. "Daniel must think very highly of you to invite you to join us."

"Yes, I do. Angela has been a great addition to my team."

The host showed them to a secluded private dining room in the rear of the restaurant where a table for three was set up and a server was already waiting for them upon their arrival. He greeted them with a tray of flutes.

"Champagne?" he inquired.

"Yes, please." Angela scooped up a glass, as did Daniel and Alejandro. Daniel hadn't told her they'd be in a private room, but she should have expected that, since that's how Daniel rolled.

Daniel held up his glass. "To a rewarding evening." He looked directly at Angela before glancing at Alejandro.

"Yes, my friend. To an intriguing night." Alejandro clinked flutes with him and Angela.

Both men were in a hurry to pull out Angela's chair, but Daniel conceded to Alejandro, much to his chagrin if the frown of his face was anything to go by. The uniformed waiter immediately came over and poured Evian into their water glasses.

"So tell me, Alejandro, what do I have to do to get you to sign with Cobb Luxury Real Estate?" Daniel wasted no time going in for the kill. Angela appreciated his forthrightness.

Alejandro laughed. "There will be time for that later, my friend." He patted Angela on the thigh. "First, let's order some wine."

He perused the menu, but Angela could see that Daniel had caught the action because disapproval was written across his face. Just as quickly it was gone.

"What looks good to you?" Daniel inquired.

Angela surveyed the wine list and everything on it was exorbitantly priced. There was no way she could ever afford to take one of her clients here, but not Daniel. He only represented the finest luxury properties, so he didn't appear shocked when the waiter approached and Alejandro ordered a five-hundred-dollar bottle of wine.

Was this really how the wealthy lived? Apparently so, because Daniel didn't blink an eye.

The waiter brought over the bottle, presented it to Alejandro before pouring him a taste. Alejandro swirled the wine around his glass, smelled it and then took a sip. He was quiet for several moments before he said, "This will do."

The waiter proceeded to pour it.

"A toast," Alejandro said when their glasses were filled. "To beauty." He turned and stared at Angela with such unmistakable lust, she blushed and quickly took a sip of her wine.

She glanced at Daniel and she could feel a leashed anger emanating from him. Would he be able to hold it in all night if Alejandro continued with his predatory treatment of her?

Thankfully, Daniel steered the conversation to business. Over their four-course dinner, they spoke of Alejandro's growing tequila business, his expansion ideas and of his potential to settle in Miami for good.

The food was absolutely delicious, but what would she expect from such a fine dining establishment? The conversation was just as stimulating. She was learning so much watching Daniel. She admired his finesse. He was a skilled negotiator and could steer people to his way of thinking. When they wanted to go left, he found a way to make sure they went right. It was a gift.

This was the side of Daniel she'd admired from afar. This was the Daniel she'd wanted to emulate. In reality, however, he was so much more than a great real estate agent with wealthy clients. He was a fascinating man. A man she was quickly starting to develop feelings for, and it wasn't just about sex. Though the attraction between them was red hot. It put her in an untenable situation, especially if he didn't share her feelings or wasn't willing to act on them.

Daniel was in awe of Angela and how well she'd handled herself the entire evening. She was professional, yet approachable, despite the fact that Alejandro wanted to take her bed. It was evident in the Colombian's eyes and in the way he made a point of touching her arm several times throughout the evening. He wanted Angela.

But he couldn't have her.

Why?

Because she was Daniel's.

He hadn't exactly made that fact known to Angela, but he suspected that she was feeling him just as much as he was her. What had happened last night in that conference room hadn't been an anomaly. She'd *allowed* the heat between them to ignite. After one kiss, all fight had gone out of her and she hadn't resisted him. Instead she'd leaned into him with those pert breasts of hers.

And he'd lost his mind, yanking up her dress, cupping her bottom and zeroing in on Angela in all her sweet glory. If he hadn't acted like an utter jerk, who knows where the night might have led? They might have gone back to his place or hers. He wouldn't have cared because then he would have finally been able to assuage the ache he'd had in his loins since they'd started working together.

Tonight was no different.

The dress she wore had to be made of some sort of spandex material because it showed him that Angela took very good care of her body. It was svelte, yet with just enough curves for him.

The problem was Alejandro was looking at her like she was his next conquest. Daniel was thankful when the Colombian got a call and had to step away from the table.

"Are you all right?" He peered into Angela's dark brown eyes.

"Of course, why wouldn't I be?"

"It's just that Alejandro is being a bit…" He paused for the right word. "Forward. And I don't like it. He shouldn't be touching you."

"Yes, he has been, but why are you so concerned?"

"You're my employee. I'd hate for any man to treat you with disrespect."

"Is that right?" she asked and the note of derision was unmistakable in her voice. "I appreciate your *concern*, but I can handle him."

"Like you handled me?"

Her eyes shot fire at him. "Why are you so upset, Daniel? Alejandro isn't the first man to like what he sees." She motioned down her body. "And he won't be the last. I've learned to have a thick skin in this business. But what I want to know is why do you care?"

Daniel was ready to tell her that he didn't want any other man looking at her, much less touching her. And he might have, if Alejandro hadn't returned. His prospective client stopped in his tracks and glanced back and forth at Daniel and Angela.

"Ah, Daniel," he said as he clapped his hand on Daniel's shoulder. "I didn't realize, my friend. If so, I wouldn't have encroached."

"Excuse me?" Daniel's brows bunched in a frown.

"I didn't realize you two were an item," Alejandro replied as he sat back down. He reached for his wineglass and liberally sipped.

"We're not," Angela stated. A little too quickly in Daniel's opinion.

"Sure, my dear." Alejandro patted her thigh and Daniel couldn't help it. He glared at him and Alejandro quickly removed his hand. "Listen, I will be in town until next week. Why don't we get together on Monday and we can talk more in depth. Sound good to you?"

Daniel nodded. "Of course."

"Then I will bid you farewell." Alejandro rose to his feet. "It's Friday night and the night is young. I am sure you lovebirds would like some alone time so I will leave you to it." He took Angela's hand and lightly kissed it. "Angela, it has been a pleasure to meet you and I hope to see you again." He shook Daniel's hand and then strode confidently from the room.

"Well, that was an interesting evening." Daniel wiped his mouth with his napkin. "Are you ready to head out? I can call the driver on the way."

"Yes." Angela was tight-lipped when she spoke and Daniel wondered what upset her. He found out when they left the restaurant and were waiting for the limo. There weren't a lot of patrons outside with them as they'd pretty much shut the restaurant down with all their stories and anecdotes.

It was just Daniel and Angela.

Alone.

When she finally turned to face him, her expression was clouded with anger. "What the hell was that back there?" she asked, pointing to the restaurant.

"What?"

"You and Alejandro acting as if I'm *either* of your property. Since he can't have me, I'm *yours* for the taking?"

Daniel chuckled. "Are you upset that Alejandro thought we're lovers?"

Angela sidled up to him until they were so close, her mouth hovered tantalizing near his. Heat uncurled low in his stomach and he felt his pulse start to race. "Yes, because it's not true," she replied.

"It could be," Daniel muttered under his breath.

"What did you say?" She was right up in his face, so close he could kiss her.

"I said," Daniel repeated louder, "that it could be." And then he hauled her hard against him and his mouth came crashing down on hers.

At first he felt her hands against his chest, resisting him, but it quickly gave way to passion and she wound her arms around his neck and kissed him back. She let him lead her, let him take control to give them both the pleasure their bodies so desperately needed.

Daniel surged backward and pushed Angela against the building and pressed his groin into her belly. She sighed, tilting her head to give him better access, allowing Daniel to slow the pace. He kissed her slowly, sensually, wetting her lips with his tongue. There was no restraint. He lost the ability to think or remember they were in public. Instead his mouth demanded and she gave.

He tugged at the clip in her updo, releasing her hair from its confines, allowing him to sink his hands into the strands. He held her head so he could explore her mouth. While his lips gloried in the feel of hers, his fingers trailed down her back and the intricate pattern at the back of her dress.

Desire stabbed through him and the world ceased to exist until they both heard tires pulling up to the driveway. Slowly, they pulled apart, but Daniel didn't let her go.

"Not here," he whispered, keeping his arm around her waist. Angela's eyes were liquid with heat and Daniel wanted to melt in them for the rest of the night *and* morning. The time for restraint was over. He wanted her in his bed.

Now.

The approaching vehicle was his limo, and his driver jumped out to open the door, but Daniel stayed him with his hand.

He opened the door for Angela himself. She didn't say a word and climbed inside.

Chapter 11

Angela had been so angry with Daniel for his and Alejandro's treatment of her that she'd been unprepared for his kiss, or the way his mouth seduced hers, commanding a response. He'd awakened a desire in her to give him everything she had. She knew it was emotional suicide to explore a path with her boss and mentor, but neither her heart nor her body would allow her to turn him down. Instead, she accepted his hand into the limo knowing what was to come.

She hadn't expected the sheer luxury that greeted her when they arrived at his building. Daniel silently rode up with her in the elevator to his penthouse. Was he as nervous as she was? If so, he didn't outwardly show it. He stood confidently across from her, smoldering all kinds of sexy that made her want to jump his bones right there and beg him to take her up against the wall.

But she didn't.

Instead, when the elevator opened and he extended his hand, she took it and walked inside his home. Her heels clicked on the bleached teakwood floor and she sucked in a deep breath at the sheer beauty. Floor-to-ceiling windows surrounded the entire place, allowing moonlight to fill the generous living areas, which were minimally decorated. The all-glass walls made the indoor living area flow seamlessly into the outdoor space, and afforded panoramic views of both the ocean and the bay. As an agent, Angela could see the appeal because it showcased the bay and ocean during the day and the magic of Miami at night. It made her feel like she was standing on the deck of a ship.

She was about to comment on the condo when she felt Daniel behind her. One arm slid around her waist, pulling her backside to his groin, while the other pushed aside her hair so he could nuzzle her neck. His mouth was on her, his lips lightly grazing her skin, his breath soft and warm.

A delicious shudder went through her and her head fell backward as Daniel's mouth trailed from her neck upward to nibble on her earlobe. She felt hot. So very hot. Her body was craving his. Her heart fluttered wildly in her chest and her pulse quickened. She didn't stop him when she felt him unzip her dress.

"Angela…" He whispered her name and she turned around in his arms.

His eyes were dark and glittering with unfettered passion. Angela couldn't help the pure excitement that danced over her as the chemistry between them exploded.

He took her face in the palm of his hands and kissed her. Her lips opened greedily and her tongue delved inside his mouth, eager to taste him. He was just as hungry as she was and he grasped her hips so purposely against his, Angela would have toppled, if not for the glass wall behind her. Her shoulders met it as Daniel continued kissing and grinding into her. His mouth savaged hers as his erection pressed into her. She wanted all that it promised and shamelessly gyrated her hips against him while sucking on his hot, probing tongue.

When he finally lifted his head from hers, she gave a slight moan of protest, but he was already pulling the straps of her dress down. He soon caught sight of her naughty secret for the evening.

"No bra? I like," he whispered, just before he began licking his way down her chest to one of her breasts. The skilled flick of his tongue sent heated sensations shooting low in her belly, and she arched against him for more, but he was already transferring his attention to her other breast. Instead of soothing the ache within her, he stoked the flames. While his tongue laved her breast, his hand lifted the hem of her dress. When he reached the tiny scrap of fabric that was her thong, he shocked her by giving it a good grip and ripping it off.

Her shocked gasp became a moan when he slid his finger inside her.

"Do you likc how that feels?" he murmured.

"Yes, yes," she moaned.

He caressed the most intimate part of her, which ached to be touched, licked and kissed. She writhed as the pads of his fingers circled the silky flesh. "Daniel…" She moaned out his name.

Did he have any idea what he was doing to her?

She was so lost in her own desire, she barely registered that he'd unbuckled and unzipped his pants until she felt them whoosh at her feet. She glanced down and smiled when she saw him push down his boxer briefs in one fell swoop. She marveled at the sheer size of him as he slid a condom on his hard length. And when she finally met his gaze, she knew instinctively what he wanted and wrapped her legs around him just as he lifted her up and surged inside her.

Daniel pushed Angela backward into the glass wall as his probing tongue found hers yet again and their mouths dueled in a searing kiss. She was so tight—so deliciously tight—that he had to rein in his desire for her and remind himself to take it slow.

He'd intended to be the debonair playboy by bringing her to his penthouse, where they'd have some champagne, then romance her into his bed upstairs. Instead, he'd seen her standing there in the moonlight overlooking the ocean and all thought had gone out the window. He only knew that if he didn't have her then, he might die.

As he moved himself inside her sweet heat, he tried to slow it down, but it was impossible. The only thing Daniel could think of was how good she felt. When he heard her gasp at his thrusts, a deep, primitive urge took over him and he grasped her hips and began driving harder into her.

"Yes, yes," Angela urged him on as her half-naked body was splayed on the wall and entwined around him. She didn't seem to care that her dress was bunched around her waist. Instead, she murmured, "Don't stop—oh yes, like that."

They were locked together in a rhythm that made Daniel shudder at just how heart-stoppingly beautiful this woman was and how she made him behave so completely out of character. Normally, he would be analyzing his actions, but all he wanted to do right now was feel. Feel her clenched around his shaft. Her back arched and she began to shudder around him. But he didn't stop moving; instead he guided them both toward sexual oblivion, and once reached, let a low, exultant cry from his lips.

Angela felt languid in Daniel's arms as he carried her upstairs to his loft bedroom and placed her on the bed. She barely had the time or the inclination to register that this room shared the minimalist decor with its counterpart downstairs. Curiosity withered, because at the moment Daniel was tossing his shirt aside to show off his toned chest, which looked as if it were made of steel. The ridges of his muscles drove out any coherent thought and made her mouth water and her knees weak.

But the best was yet to come. She licked her lips in eager anticipation when he began stripping off the boxer briefs that had molded to his shaft. She'd caught a glimpse downstairs right before he'd taken her in spectacular fashion up against the glass wall, but now Angela drank in the sight of him. Daniel was a fine-looking specimen of a man, and she was certainly looking forward to spending more time with him.

The sheer force of their chemistry had frightened her, because she hadn't envisioned they wouldn't make it to a bed their first time together. But they'd been circling each other for a while and ever since he'd made her come last night in the conference room, she couldn't deny the powerful attraction between them.

And now here she was lying on his platform king-size bed with her dress around her waist, but instead of being embarrassed, she rose to her knees and shimmied her way out of it, tossing it onto the floor with Daniel's articles of clothing, then continuing to strip until she was just as naked as he was. He grinned as he strode toward her wearing nothing but a smile and displaying one impressive erection.

He met her in the middle of the bed and they tumbled backward. Angela shivered as he took her in his arms again. His fingertips lightly skated over her back in soft, light caresses. She sensed he was going to take his time arousing her, but Angela had tasted pleasure and was greedy for more of it.

Their attraction to each other was wild, crazy and definitely complicated. Tomorrow would be a whole different ball game, but tonight…tonight she would allow herself to enjoy the moment and be with Daniel before reality crept in.

He stroked her cheek. "Stop thinking," he whispered, "and just feel."

Angela's chin came up so she could kiss him, softly, sweetly, and then harder and deeper. Daniel groaned, but he didn't stop kissing her. Instead their tongues mated in a sensual dance that left Angela breathless and heady. His mouth continued its journey to her neck and throat. His breath was hot and warm and she instantly responded to him, enjoying the feel of his tongue and weight of his lips on her. So much so that when she felt the rasp of his jaw against her breast, she trembled. And when he caught one of her nipples between his teeth and began sucking and licking, she let out a sharp cry of pleasure.

"Like that?" he inquired.

"Mmm… I love it. Do it again."

He laughed, but did exactly as she requested and began tonguing one breast and then the other with light, swift flicks of his tongue. Angela marveled at just how good Daniel could make her feel. She'd had other lovers and knew good sex, but Daniel was different. With him she felt something other than desire. Something she couldn't quite name or perhaps wasn't ready to. Instead, she just let go.

One of Daniel's hands snaked its way from holding her to skim the soft flesh between her thighs. A cloud of desire, of wanting, hung over Angela as she watched, waited for him to touch her there. But instead his fingers danced over her thighs and down to the back of her knees.

"Please…" she murmured, squirming underneath him. It was shameless to beg, but she needed Daniel's hand, his mouth, his shaft inside her. And at the moment, she would take whatever she could get.

And when he finally graced the triangle of curls that waited for his touch with his fingertips, she sighed with contentment. When he slid one finger and then another inside her, she let out a low purr. She rocked her body against him, eager for more.

A large hand splayed over her stomach, stilling her, and he lifted his head and said, "I've got you." Seconds later, his head was diving between her thighs and he was throwing her legs over his shoulders.

Her head fell back against the bed when his fingers and tongue moved in parallel penetration inside her. He knew how to evoke unbearable pleasure, and her belly tightened and her thighs quivered uncontrollably. He explored every inch of her. There was no part he didn't coax, until finally her orgasm came deep and intense.

"Daniel!" she screamed.

Only then did he retreat abruptly, returning only after he'd rolled on a condom. His eyes held hers fast as his hands grasped her hips, holding her firmly as he eased inside her, slowly at first, inch by delicious inch before withdrawing. Angela sucked in a deep breath just as he thrust forward again, burying himself to the hilt inside her.

She moaned loudly when he brushed her hair aside so he could kiss, then suck, her neck. She cried out in pleasure, her nails scraping back and forth across the linens as sensation after sensation built inside her, growing tighter and tighter as he moved deep within her. She locked her legs around his waist, her inner muscles clenching around him in an attempt to hold him still, but that merely caused Daniel to drive faster and harder into her.

Angela was desperate for him to release her from the torment, but at the same time she didn't want it to end. Her mouth opened to speak, but then the dam burst and a tidal wave swept over her. A feeling of immense satisfaction and contentment enveloped her just as Daniel gave a loud shout as he, too, reached the peak of exquisite delight.

Daniel levered himself up onto his elbow and surveyed Angela. Her hair was spread out gloriously across his pillow, and his heart leaped.

How had this woman mesmerized him so? What was it about her that made him reckless, with no thought or care about tomorrow? When he was with Angela, reason went out the window and all he was left with was a desire so strong, he showed no finesse when they'd coupled the first time.

It had been hot, fast, but oh so satisfying. He'd never felt this way in any of his other sexual experiences. So why was being with Angela so intense? He'd felt driven earlier to take her. There'd been a primal, almost animal need in him to mate and possess her.

And he had.

He'd lingered over every luxurious womanly curve, but he couldn't wait to explore her in even more intimate detail, to feel all that there could be between them. He would make love to her again as if he had all the time in the world, but for now he would let her sleep.

Chapter 12

Eventually, when she woke up later that morning, Angela was famished. They'd certainly worked up an appetite, making love several times throughout the morning and night.

"Do you intend to feed me?" she asked, elbowing Daniel in the side. "Or am I merely here to sate your ravenous desires?"

Daniel turned on his side and gave her a dazzling smile. "My ravenous desires? I'd say someone shared my enthusiasm." He reached for the sheet between them and lowered it so he could tweak her nipple between his thumb and forefinger.

"Hey!" She smacked his hand away. "Don't start something you can't finish. I'm hungry."

His eyes darkened. "Oh yeah? So am I."

"Down, tiger. I need food."

"All right." He rose from the bed and padded unashamedly naked out of the room. He returned several moments later with his phone. In their hasty encounter last night, his pants were still on the living room floor. "Let's order in. What do you fancy?"

After they'd ordered, Daniel threw on a pair of jogging pants and selected a Millionaire Moguls T-shirt from his closet for Angela to wear, which, she noticed, was so neat it was color-coded. Then he headed to the kitchen to make them coffee.

Angela followed behind him. As she did, she looked around the penthouse. In the light of day, she saw that Daniel didn't have much in the way of family photos or personal memorabilia. The only decoration was the odd abstract piece of art and sculptures. About the only item that was in abundance was an extensive library of books. "Where are all your photos?" she inquired.

"Of whom?"

"Of your family. Your friends. Don't you have any?"

Daniel busied himself with adding water to his Keurig machine and procuring mugs for each of them from the overhead cabinets. He placed the first pod in the machine and let it percolate. "Of course I do, I just choose not to display them. I like a clean slate."

Angela wondered if that was the real reason. She'd never seen a home so bare of personality. Was there something Daniel was trying to hide or didn't want to show the rest of the world? Or perhaps something or someone he wanted to forget? His penthouse could use some warmth, and if she happened to become more of a fixture here, she would do something about it.

Daniel handed her the first mug of coffee. "And you? What's your apartment like?" He added another pod to the Keurig to make himself a cup.

"My place has lots of big bold colors, plants and paintings."

"Much like you," Daniel mused. "You're very bold and expressive."

"Yes, I am. There's nothing wrong with having some individuality."

"Sounds like that's been a problem for you in the past," Daniel said as he reached for the finished mug of coffee and brought it to his lips.

How had he picked up on that?

She shrugged. "My parents are conformists. Everything by the book. And I just dance to the beat of my own drum."

"I would say that makes you special."

"Aw, shucks." Angela laughed. "If I didn't know any better I'd think you liked me."

"I do." His deep brown eyes fixed on her and moved down her body. There was an invisible web of attraction building between them again. It made Angela feel as if she were standing stark naked in front of him. A thrill of arousal caused heat to begin pooling between her legs, flooding her with desire.

As quickly as it flared to life, it was extinguished as the doorbell rang, breaking the trance between them. Daniel placed his mug on the counter and sauntered toward the door.

Angela watched him intently, knowing that had it not been for the doorbell, they would have been on the floor of the living room fanning those sparks into a raging inferno.

Five minutes later, they were sitting on his bed, pigging out on crab Benedict, wheat toast, a fruit medley and the best fresh-squeezed orange juice she'd ever had, all from a nearby eatery.

"How did you manage to get them to deliver?" she inquired, stuffing her mouth with eggs.

"I'm Daniel Cobb."

Angela nearly choked on her food. "Did anyone ever tell you you're just a little bit cocky?"

He gave her one of his irresistible grins. "I may have been told that a time or two, but I don't mind it, if it shows I'm confident."

Angela took another forkful of her crab dish. "So, Mr. Cocky, how do we handle this?" She motioned back and forth between them.

His grin quickly dissipated. "You sure do cut to the chase."

"Well, I've never found myself in a situation like this," Angela responded. "So forgive me if I'm a little out of my element."

"Sleeping with a man you're attracted to?" he offered.

It was more than that and he knew it. He was trying to make light of the awkward situation they found themselves in. Angela applauded him for trying, but she didn't know her way out of it any more than he did. It's why she went on the offensive. Find out what he was thinking first so she could react accordingly. She didn't want to be the one to lay her feelings bare, not knowing what he might say in return. The last time she'd done that, it hadn't worked out too well.

"Sleeping with my boss," she finally responded.

He nodded quietly and sipped on his juice, having finished off his breakfast in record time. She could see the wheels of his mind spinning, figuring out what to say, what to do. "Who says we have to do anything?"

Her brows furrowed. "What do you mean?"

He shrugged. "Why can't we just enjoy each other for however long it lasts? Because clearly staying away from each other hasn't worked."

Angela thought back to the last couple of weeks. From the moment Daniel started mentoring her, the attraction between them had slowly simmered, flaring to life in the limo after the Heat game and then combusting in the Cobb conference room. They'd both tried unsuccessfully to suppress the attraction, and all they'd accomplished was to become so frustrated that their first coupling had been a frenzied one against the glass wall. Angela doubted she'd ever look at his apartment without remembering their passionate encounter.

"I don't know," she replied to his suggestion. "I need to think about it."

Daniel reached across the space between them, grabbed her plate and placed it on the nightstand behind him. "What's there to think about? You want me and I want you. The sex between us is raw and intense. Hell, it's amazing! Even you have to admit it." His dark eyes stared into hers. "Why shouldn't we continue to see each other?"

Angela swallowed hard at his frank assessment. He was laying it all bare in black and white. But she was still hesitant. "How would we act at work?" It was one scenario she'd never worked out when she'd considered a one-night stand with him.

"Same as before," Daniel said. "I'll continue to mentor you."

"As I continue to get you off?"

Daniel hissed, not liking her comment, and before she knew it Angela was flat on her back with Daniel poised above her. "I would think that would be mutual," he replied. "But in case you need further evidence of just how much you enjoyed my getting *you* off…" Daniel lifted the T-shirt she was wearing, parted her legs and then lowered his head.

The first flick of his tongue caused Angela to arch off the bed, but Daniel gently eased her down with the palm of his hand while his tongue took liberties with her already-sensitive flesh. He teased and stroked her with effortless ease, tipping her nearly to the edge of her orgasm, then drawing her back, time and time again.

Frustration and excitement grew to a fever pitch until Angela was begging him to take her. Only then did Daniel let out a long laugh, lifting his head. "Do you want to amend your earlier comment?" he asked, lightly blowing on her clitoris.

"Y-yes," Angela stammered. "Now, for Christ's sake, give me what I want."

"And what do you want?" He drew circles with his tongue around her clit.

"You. Inside me," she said unapologetically.

Daniel eased the jogging pants down his thighs and reached for yet another condom. They'd already gone through a box. She took it from him, and her fingers worked magic as she slowly slid the condom down his hard length. Then he was back in place, threading his fingers through her silken mass of hair and giving her exactly what she wanted.

He lifted her hips and positioned himself so his shaft slid inside her. Angela purred. Damn! Why did she make him feel this way? So wanton, so out of control. He was losing his grip on the situation. Instead he focused on doing incredibly wicked things to her and proving she was powerless to resist him.

Daniel's mouth crashed down on hers and his tongue glided into her hot mouth. He wanted to show Angela that there was no way she was walking away from what they shared. It was hot and passionate. The softness of her body merged with his, and it was impossible to know where he ended and she began.

His body was consumed by a burning need that only Angela could quench. He dragged his mouth away from hers long enough to suck on one plump breast. Desire was coiling inside him, threatening to overtake him, but he didn't want it to be over with quickly. He wanted to make it last.

Slowly he thrust and withdrew, reveling in how tight and wet she was. The feeling of being inside her was so exquisite that he groaned aloud.

"Yes, Daniel, yes," she moaned, gyrating her hips underneath him.

Daniel didn't quicken the pace. He let the pressure and tension build inside them, thrusting in and out with agonizing slowness until finally she sobbed, crying out his name. Only then did he move quicker, harder and deeper until he reached the hilt, and when he did, he shattered into a million pieces.

On Sunday, after he'd met with several members of the Millionaire Moguls Club at a local martini bar in an effort to solidify support for Joshua, Daniel sat alone at the bar with a drink to clear his head. It wouldn't be easy dethroning Ashton, but he'd given his word he would help. On the other hand, he would much rather be at his place with Angela.

She'd been a fiery tigress in his bed. He'd spent the entire day laying with her yesterday after their first sexual encounter had him aching for more of her. He hadn't known it would be that way. Hadn't known he'd feel the intense desire he felt when they were together. Angela surpassed any of his previous relationships. Since Mia, he'd kept women at arm's length because he was afraid of putting his heart on the line and being rejected, so when this relationship ran its course—which was an inevitability given that Daniel didn't do long-term relationships— Angela would become the yardstick he measured every other woman against, because she was the woman who'd made him *feel* something.

He was so deep in thought that he didn't realize he'd been joined by someone until a smooth voice slid over him like syrup. A voice that took him back to another place in time.

He glanced up from his drink to find Farrah Davenport, his ex-girlfriend, sitting beside him. "Farrah." He inclined his head and returned to sipping his drink.

"Is that all I get after we shared two thrilling months together?" she inquired.

Turning again, Daniel stared at her. Farrah was stunningly beautiful and was of mixed African American and West Indian heritage. She had flawless skin, expressive eyes and a body that most women would kill for and that she'd used to get what she wanted—his wallet. The only things Farrah cared about were whether he was good in bed and whether he could support her lifestyle. Too bad he figured that out after he'd shelled out thousands during their short-lived dating stint.

"You're looking well," Daniel said after his slow perusal. Farrah was dressed in a jumpsuit with a neckline that damn near plunged to her waist, showing off her spectacular cleavage. Daniel could appreciate the package even though Angela was far more beautiful in his opinion, both inside and out.

"I'm glad you noticed." She eased herself on the bar stool as best she could without her breasts falling out of the jumpsuit and faced him with her legs crossed. It wasn't lost on him that she was pulling out all the stops to prove she could still hold his interest.

He gave her a withering glance. "Isn't that what you're looking for in that getup?"

Farrah laughed, throwing back her head so that her long flowing mane of hair, thanks to a thousand-dollar Brazilian weave, could cascade down her back. She truly was a piece of work. There was nothing real about her. Everything was for show. Why had he never seen it before?

"I just threw on this old thing," Farrah replied. "I'm meeting some friends for dinner."

"Don't let me keep you."

She frowned. "You're not. They're late." Then she chuckled to herself. "Usually I'm the one fashionably late. Anyway, what are you doing here?"

"Having a drink." Daniel wasn't interested in giving her any details. Farrah was a notorious gossip, so whatever he said would make the rounds in Miami society, blogs and social media.

"Alone? The Daniel I know likes having a beautiful woman on his arm."

"And who's to say that I don't have a woman?" His mind instantly went to Angela.

"Then where is she? Doesn't she know she can't let a lion like you out of his cage?"

Daniel turned to glare at her but not before downing the last of his scotch. "We're not doing this, Farrah."

"Doing what?"

"Acting like you care about who I'm seeing."

"Why are you so afraid to share?" she countered. "If she's so amazing, I'd think you'd be raving about her, but since you're not it tells me that nothing has changed."

"Changed? What the hell does that mean?"

She scooted off the bar stool and placed her hands on her slender hips, studying him. "You know the reason we broke up, Daniel. And though I do like a certain lifestyle, it wasn't just about the money. I feel sorry for the poor mouse you're seeing because she has no idea the world of hurt she's gotten herself into."

After Farrah had gone, Daniel thought about her parting comment.

She was wrong. The real reason they'd split was her rampant desire for money. He loved spoiling his women and giving them trinkets, taking them out to the best restaurants and on fabulous vacations, but at the end of the day, she'd been nothing more than a gold digger, plain and simple.

Now, Angela…

She was different. She had him wondering what it would be like if they were a couple. When she'd left his place earlier she'd been noncommittal, and he wasn't sure whether she wanted to see him again. He certainly wanted to see her again, could picture her becoming a frequent bed partner, but Angela was playing hard to get.

And he didn't like it.

He was used to being the one in charge, but this time he had to follow her lead. This time he would have to wait for her to make the first move.

Chapter 13

"What a great venue," Angela gushed as she and Denise walked the Mezz, a venue known for weddings, bar mitzvahs and quinceañeras.

The coordinator was highlighting the seven-thousand-square-foot venue with wraparound floor-to-ceiling windows, modern decor and state-of-the-art sound system that they could use for her parents' anniversary party, but Angela was focused on the bold wallpapers and distinctive backdrops in the Plum Room.

"This is it," Angela said.

"I don't know," Denise replied. "I was thinking something a little more traditional."

Angela rolled her eyes. There it was again. The key difference between her and her family. Sometimes she felt as if she'd been snatched at birth and given to the wrong family because she didn't share their same thought processes.

"Why not switch it up a bit?" Angela said. "I'm sure the Mezz can create whatever feel we want. Isn't that right?" She turned to the coordinator.

"Oh, absolutely," the young woman replied. "We can make miracles happen with our draping, uplighting and decor."

"Sign us up," Angela responded.

"Angela! A word, please." Denise spoke harshly.

As soon as Angela walked over, Denise grabbed her by the arm and led her several feet away. "I didn't know this was a dictatorship. I thought you wanted my input. And this," she said as she motioned around the room, "is not our parents."

"Well, this," Angela said as she mimicked her sister's hand movements, "is what I like and since I'm the one footing the bill, I see no reason not to do something unique and special for *our* parents. You're not the only one with good taste."

Denise stepped back, obviously appalled by Angela's forthrightness, but Angela didn't care. Her voice was going to be heard, and she wasn't going to be railroaded into doing things Denise's way. Everyone may have been dancing to her baby sister's tune since her arrival on this earth, but that time was over and done with.

"Very well," Denise said. "Then just let me know when my help is required."

"I'll do that."

As she drove back to her apartment later that evening, Angela was dog-tired. She hadn't gotten much in the way of sleep the last two nights thanks to Daniel and touring several venues today with Denise. Friday night's dinner with Alejandro had flowed into Saturday night in Daniel's arms. By the time she and Daniel had finally come up for air, it was late. Daniel had tempted her to stay Saturday night because she had nothing to wear but the clothes she'd come in.

But clothes hadn't mattered much because they'd spent most of their thirty-six hours together naked, wrapped in each other's arms and making love endlessly. Angela hadn't known it was possible to be so entranced, but Daniel had her under some sort of spell and she'd been unable to say no to him. She'd always thought herself a strong woman, but she hadn't felt very strong this weekend.

Instead, he'd taken her to new heights over and over again in bed. She'd sobbed his name and begged him to take her on numerous occasions. Angela blushed at the memory. And now he wanted to continue their relationship indefinitely, until one or the both of them called it quits. She wasn't sure how she felt about it.

Working together and sleeping together day after day could make life very complicated at the office. Look at what happened when they'd tried staying away from each other. They'd both been miserable. But if she continued seeing him, what did that mean? Would the sexual tension that had been between them remain, or would sex with her become mundane? Would he toss her away as soon as he was bored?

Could she handle that?

On the other hand, if she didn't take the risk, would she always wonder what could have been if she'd followed her heart and not her head?

Monday at work, Angela was a nervous wreck wondering where Daniel was, what he was doing and how he would treat her. She was so anxious that even Myrna commented.

"Are you all right?" she inquired when Angela kept glancing at the door as she stood in front of her reception desk chatting about their weekends.

"Y-yes, why do you ask?"

It was midmorning and she'd yet to see Daniel. Was he avoiding her? Was he regretting being with her? Or was she being paranoid? Perhaps he had a showing that day. She was afraid to ask Myrna for fear she'd be called out. The wily receptionist had already warned her about Daniel's reputation.

"You just seem a little jittery is all, not your usual self."

"Probably too much coffee."

And then her heart began to speed up as if she'd had several cups of espresso when Daniel sauntered through the front door. He gave them both a casual glance and said, "Good morning." And then he strolled to his office without a backward glance at Angela.

She tried not to be offended, but after everything they'd shared he'd basically just ignored her.

"Is something going on?" Myrna said when Angela's eyes were still glued on Daniel and his now-closed door.

"Hmm...?" Angela turned to face her.

"You and Daniel?" Myrna shook her head. "Please say it isn't so. You've read the gossip blogs. Seen the magazines. Mr. Cobb is excellent at what he does, but he's a notorious ladies' man. You would do well to watch out for him."

"Nothing's going on between me and Daniel," Angela replied. "He's my mentor, nothing more."

"I fear for you, Angela. You're treading on dangerous territory. You would be wise to heed my advice and steer clear of the boss."

"That would be pretty hard since I'm shadowing him and working with him on a couple of listings."

"Forewarned is forearmed." Myrna shrugged. "Don't say I didn't warn you."

But it was too late. Angela was already starting to develop feelings for Daniel, and the harder she tried to push them down the more they kept resurfacing.

Daniel breathed a sigh of relief once he was behind the closed door of his office. He'd had a very productive breakfast meeting with Alejandro. He'd finally convinced the Colombian to sign on with Cobb Luxury Real Estate, but not after Alejandro had razzed him about his relationship with Angela.

Alejandro had made it very clear that if Daniel didn't know how to handle such a woman, he did. Daniel had told his new client in no uncertain terms that Angela was his and was off-limits. It had taken everything within Daniel to walk by Angela and not pull her into his arms and give her a proper kiss. It had been twenty-four hours, and he needed a hit of Angela.

As much as he'd love to strip her naked and feast on her for hours, he had a job to do. He not only had to steer Cobb Luxury Real Estate to the stratosphere, he also had to keep his word and tutor Angela on how to court and keep wealthy clientele.

So he was going to have to put his attraction to her on the shelf. Or at least until after 5:00 p.m., when he fully intended to make a pitch to her on just how good it could be between them if she allowed nature to take its course.

Angela never made it back to the office after her showings that day and instead headed home. It had been a long day and all she wanted to do was kick off her shoes and curl up with a glass of wine and some takeout that she'd picked up along the way.

However, what she found was Daniel leaning against the door frame outside her apartment building in dark jeans and a black V-neck shirt, looking sexy as hell.

She halted her steps, unsure of what to do. She'd never expected him to show up at her place, not after his indifference toward her earlier at the office. But he had, so she would have to face him head-on. She resumed walking toward him and he straightened his stance.

"Good evening," Daniel said when she approached.

"Daniel."

"I was hoping we could talk," he said. "I brought wine." He held up a bottle of red wine that Angela was sure cost a mint.

"All right. C'mon in." Angela inclined her head toward the front door.

As the elevator climbed to the sixth floor, silence hung between them. Angela didn't want to speak first. She wanted to hear what Daniel had to say, considering he'd made the effort to seek her out tonight.

Blessedly the doors sprang open and they walked down the corridor to her apartment. "This is me," she said, stopping at her door. Angela didn't have the chance to be fearful of how Daniel would view her apartment as she'd been on their first encounter.

She flicked on the switch, flooding the kitchen and open living area with light. Daniel walked inside and surveyed her home. She looked at it through Daniel's eyes. The kitchen was renovated with granite countertops, stainless steel appliances and maple cabinets, and the living room had a comfy sofa, a flat-screen and a small balcony with a view of Miami. Still, it couldn't compare to his penthouse.

He turned to face her. "Nice place."

She laughed as she removed her high heels one at a time and placed them on the shoe rack near her front door. "You don't have to say that, Daniel."

"I mean it," he said, walking back toward her. "Where's your bottle opener?" He brushed past her in the small corridor and stepped into the kitchen.

She sucked in a breath. "Drawer to the left of the stove. If you don't mind I'd like to get out of these clothes."

Daniel's brows rose.

And she quickly added, "Into something more comfortable."

"Of course. By all means."

While he busied himself uncorking the wine, Angela rushed into her bedroom and closed the door. She rested her back against it, reminding herself to calm down. So what if Daniel was in her home? She could handle the situation. She was in control.

Or so she told herself as she undressed, then put on her favorite pair of yoga pants and a tank top. Deep down, she wasn't sure she believed it. He'd caught her off guard with his unplanned visit.

When she emerged five minutes later, Daniel had found the wineglasses in the cupboard and poured them each a glass. He handed her one when she came forward. "Thank you," she said as she accepted the wine.

He held out his glass. "Cheers."

She lightly tapped hers to his. "Cheers."

She took a long sip to fortify herself for the conversation. Then she moved toward the living room and made herself comfortable on the microsuede sofa she'd bought several years ago on sale. "So you want to tell me why you stopped by unannounced?" she asked, tucking her feet under her.

"Absolutely." Daniel followed her and instead of sitting in the adjacent chair, he sat beside her on the sofa. "We needed to talk."

"I think you were very clear with your intentions," Angela asked, "and I believe I asked you for some time to think about it."

"And I," he responded, "felt like you might need some convincing."

"Is that right?"

He smiled broadly and Angela's insides turned to mush at his irrepressible grin. "Oh yes, and I'm here to offer you a proposition."

Her interest was piqued. "I'm intrigued. Do go on."

"Well, I think it's pretty obvious how attracted we are to each other."

Angela didn't attempt to refute that, because he was right. When they were within a few feet of each other, sparks crackled between them. Even now she could feel his energy pulling her toward him.

"And as much as we've tried to fight it, ignore it, it's still there," Daniel continued. "We have to see where this goes, Angela. If we don't, we'll drive ourselves crazy. But I recognize you're hesitant given our working relationship. So I propose that we spend the weekend together in Key West. We'll either get our fill of each other and go our separate ways or we'll decide to continue the relationship. What do you say?"

Daniel watched with bated breath for Angela's answer. He'd thought about this solution to their quandary all day. And this was the best he'd come up with. They could sex each other like crazy for an entire weekend and get it out of their system and decide to end their affair. Or they could decide to continue a discreet relationship behind closed doors.

Either way, he'd get to have Angela in his arms again.

He'd tried unsuccessfully to get the woman out of his mind since she'd left his apartment yesterday morning to meet her sister. She'd clouded his thoughts until he'd finally decided he had to do something about it. He was now determined to convince her that they needed to spend time together and figure out what was between them.

Daniel placed his wineglass on the cocktail table in front of him and reached for one of Angela's hands. "Don't deny yourself, deny us, because you're scared. I know we're on uncharted territory here, but there's something between us. You must feel it like I do."

He watched her bring her wineglass to her mouth for a sip and realized her hand was shaking. Daniel wished he were that glass. Wished he could take her lips with his and suck the sweet juices off them. But he didn't want to come on too strong or she would pull away.

He released her hand and rose to his feet. "Think about it."

"You've certainly given me a lot to consider," she finally said.

"I know, but when I feel strongly about something, I go after it."

"And you want me?"

Those beautiful brown eyes of hers looked up at him expectantly. "I think that's obvious, or I wouldn't be here. And I believe you want me, too. So think about my proposition. I've chartered a private plane to take us to Key West on Friday morning, so I hope I'm not going alone. But the choice is yours."

She was silent, but rose and walked him to the door. He opened it, then stopped and turned back around. Angela was standing nervously behind him in that darn tank top that showed him she wasn't wearing a bra underneath. Her nipples were visible and protruding, and Daniel lost his head.

He reached for her, circling his arm around her waist. His body pressed into hers and then his lips coaxed hers open. She gasped at the urgency of his demanding kiss, and that allowed Daniel to ease his tongue into her mouth. He explored her sweet mouth slowly, tasting, teasing, sucking and nibbling. He wanted to remind her of just how good it was between them and how good it could be again if she only gave in to the desire she felt for him.

When he finally pulled away, her lips were swollen from his kisses and her eyes were dazed. "I await your answer," he said.

And then he left.

He had to. Otherwise, he'd be taking her up against the wall as he'd done their first time together at his penthouse, and he didn't want that. He wanted to take his time making sweet love to her until the only people who existed in the world were the two of them.

Chapter 14

Angela knew her answer to Daniel's proposition even before he'd left her apartment several days ago, but she'd made him wait. However, today was Thursday and she'd have to let him know her decision one way or another. And she would be able to do so in private because Daniel had arranged a showing of one of the condos at the downtown development they were working on together for that afternoon. She was sure it had been done purposely so they wouldn't have an audience.

She'd worn a simple nude sheath and added a long, dangling gold necklace and sparkling gold peep-toe pumps. Angela knew she looked good. No, she looked hot, and there was no way Daniel wouldn't take notice.

She was already on-site at the condo before Daniel arrived because her appointment had ended early, giving her time to arrive for setup. She'd told Daniel's assistant, Mary, not to come out for staging, leaving them completely alone until their prospect arrived.

She'd just finished setting out the fine china, champagne flutes and finger foods she'd picked up from Daniel's favorite eatery and was using the smart device that came with the house to open all the blinds when he arrived.

He stopped midstride when he saw her. "Angela. You're here early." He closed the door behind him.

"I had a little free time," she responded, "so I took care of everything."

"And Mary?"

Angela stared at him boldly. "Isn't here. It's just us."

"That's fortuitous."

"Yes, it gives us time to talk."

"Am I going to like your answer?" Daniel asked, walking forward and placing his portfolio on the counter. "Perhaps I should uncork this champagne and have a glass to prepare myself."

"No need." Angela shook her head, tossing her mane of hair from side to side. "You'll like my answer."

"Which is?"

"Yes."

"Yes to?"

"Yes to the weekend in Key West. Yes to the two of us until it ends."

He released a long sigh and then laughed. "Could you have led with that?"

She smirked. "And what fun would that have been? What do they say? Anticipation makes it all the more sweet?"

"I'm going to look forward to a little revenge, Ms. Trainor." Daniel strode toward her and planted a swift kiss on her lips. "Wait until the shoe is on the other foot. I'll have you begging for it."

"You think so?"

"Oh, I know so," Daniel replied. "And I'm going to enjoy every minute of watching you squirm waiting for my touch, for my kiss, for my—"

Of all times for the doorbell to ring.

Daniel released her and strode to the door to let in their client.

She pulled herself together and smoothed down her dress. But she couldn't stop the voice inside her head.

What the hell have I just gotten myself into?

Daniel spared no expense with the plane he'd chartered to take them to Key West on Friday morning. Angela wasn't sure what everyone in the office might be thinking with both her and Daniel absent, and she didn't care. She was just going to live in the moment. She'd never flown in a private plane and was impressed with its deluxe interior. Decorated in black and cream with richly textured wool carpeting, the five-seater plane had embossed leather details and its own bathroom.

"Comfortable?" Daniel asked once they were seated and the plane had taken off for their short flight.

"Yes, this is lovely."

"Well, I try to impress."

Angela frowned. "You know, you didn't have to go through all this trouble. I would have been just as happy driving down to the Keys."

"A three-hour drive? What fun would that have been?" Daniel inquired. "No, this is far better. Champagne?"

"Please."

He poured them flutes from the already-uncorked

champagne that had been sitting at the beverage bar. "To a great weekend."

An hour later, they disembarked. A limo was waiting to whisk them off to a two-bedroom beach cottage in Key West with whimsical painted furniture, locally inspired art and French doors. Angela was surprised that Daniel selected something quaint and charming and not over the top as she'd come to expect from him.

"What?" he asked when she stared at him.

"I'm just surprised by the cottage."

"You don't love this place?" Daniel inquired. "Look at that view." He pointed to the beach, which was steps away from the rear of the cottage.

Angela shook her head and her ponytail bounced from side to side. "I *love* it." She beamed as she thought of the Adirondack chairs facing the Gulf of Mexico. "I just thought you'd pick something a little more ostentatious."

"Well, I can be romantic," Daniel said, coming toward her and hauling her into his arms. "I wanted this weekend to be special and about the two of us."

"Well, you achieved that. So what did you have in store for us today?"

A wicked grin spread across his full lips.

"Besides that."

"Well, after we unpack, I thought we'd stroll around Duval Street, take in the sights and sounds, maybe share a slice of key lime pie and watch the sunset."

Angela smiled. "Daniel Cobb, you continue to amaze me."

That's exactly what Daniel wanted. He wanted to show Angela how good life could be as *his* woman. He loved spoiling her as he usually did in most of his relationships, but if he had to admit it, he'd taken more care with this trip.

Angela had been right. Normally, he would have picked one of the luxury resorts where they'd be waited on hand and foot, but something told him that Angela might appreciate a more subtle approach. Not that he intended for it all to be casual. He had a few tricks up his sleeve to wow her.

After they'd unpacked and freshened up, he shocked her by having her hop on the back of a scooter he'd rented for the weekend and they headed into town. The streets were bustling with locals and tourists, and they slipped in and out of stores hawking souvenirs, art, collectibles and other Key West treasures.

They paused long enough for Daniel to buy Angela a ring she'd been admiring through the window. It was a gold band with a pearl and intricate diamonds surrounding it. It was delicate and looked great on her hand.

Eventually they stopped at Kermit's for lunch and what Daniel felt was the best key lime pie in town. As the afternoon drew to a close, they meandered back to the pier, where he had a surprise in store for her.

"What are we doing here?" Angela inquired.

He pointed to the sailboat. "We're going on a sunset cruise. C'mon." He grabbed her hand. "Or we'll be late." They walked down the plank toward the boat, where a man dressed in a sailor's outfit greeted them.

"Mr. Cobb, welcome aboard." He helped Angela and then Daniel up onto the boat.

"Are we here alone?" Angela asked. "I saw a couple of other boats that were filling up with people."

"Yes, ma'am," the man answered before Daniel could. "Mr. Cobb chartered the entire boat for your use to watch the sunset. Dinner will be served at seven p.m. sharp as per your request, Mr. Cobb."

"Thank you." Daniel inclined his head and then looked at Angela. "I hope this meets with your approval."

"My approval? Daniel!" She jumped into his arms and he caught her. She wrapped her long legs around his middle. "This is incredible and I can't wait to watch the sunset with you."

The joy emanating from her was infectious, and Daniel couldn't remember a time when he'd felt so relaxed and so carefree. What was Angela doing to him?

Later, once they'd made their way back to the cottage and sat wrapped in throws on loungers to stargaze, Angela realized Daniel had her under his spell and she wasn't sure she wanted to come out of it. She'd tried to deny what was happening, but how could she when he'd done all this? Arranging a romantic sunset cruise and the subsequent delicious seafood dinner of Maine lobster, blue crab and oysters was the single most romantic thing a man had ever done for her. He was surpassing her hopes for this weekend and it had only just begun.

"Did you enjoy the day?" Daniel turned on his side to face her on the lounger.

Angela nodded, staring back at him. "I was just thinking it couldn't get any better than this."

"Oh, I was thinking it could," Daniel said and before she could protest, he had drawn her across the short distance and had her sprawled across his hard body on his lounger. He kissed her long and deep. It was an unrelentingly thorough kiss as he claimed her. Made her his.

A moan escaped Angela's lips and she wrapped her arms around him. Heated excitement coursed through her at feeling his hard loins underneath her. His hands were everywhere, exploring the length of her body, molding and shaping her breasts and curves as if he were memorizing every inch of her.

Angela's senses swam even more when Daniel shifted beneath her until they were sitting upright. His hands traveled under her top, lifting it over her head. Then his mouth was kissing the hollow at the base of her throat while his fingers deftly unhooked and removed her bra, leaving her naked from the waist up.

He threaded his hands through her hair and searched her face. "I want you like this. Carefree and naked under the stars." Then his head descended and he took one nipple in his mouth and sucked.

"Ah." Angela threw her head back, holding his head in place as he paid homage to one breast and then the other with his skillful tongue, coaxing, teasing and tantalizing her until she was whimpering.

She didn't even realize he'd moved until she was lying on her back on the lounger and felt her shorts and panties being tugged down. In seconds she was naked.

Even though it was dark, she could see Daniel's gaze darken, then he lowered himself to his knees on the lounger to the silky mound at the junction of her thighs that begged for his touch. She felt his fingertips first, caressing her, testing her to see if she was ready for the ultimate intimacy.

She rose up on one of her elbows to watch him and answered his unasked question. "Yes."

Then she felt his tongue as it stroked, then circled that tiny nub until it swelled for him. He was so skilled and practiced at coaxing a response from her that when he sucked on it a strangled cry escaped her lips.

"Daniel!"

She was lost. She couldn't think about anything except the sweet feeling of Daniel's mouth on her and how she wanted *all* of him inside her. She tried reaching for him to bring him toward her, but he caught both her hands and pinned them to her sides as he continued to feast on her.

He lifted his head only for a second to remind her of her earlier taunt. "Remember when you said you'd never beg? And I said you'd eat those words?"

Angela remembered that all-too-familiar taunt and instead of resisting, she eased back on the lounger and took her punishment. And oh, what a sweet surrender it was.

When Daniel was sure that Angela was fully satisfied after three orgasms, only then did he take off the linen pants he'd been wearing and join her on the lounger. She was so passionate that he couldn't wait to be inside her.

"Now it's time for my fun," Daniel said, brushing damp hair from her face.

"Oh yeah?" she asked. "And what would you like?"

"You on top." He handed her a condom.

"I think I can arrange that." Angela slid from beside him until she was sitting astride him. She reached down and grasped his growing member in her hands, rolled a condom on and then led him inside her. She sank down onto him as her entire sweet body closed around him. She clutched his face to her bosom, and the hardened tips of her peaks brushed against him.

It was such sweet torture and Daniel wanted more. He leaned back. "That's right, baby. Ride me."

And she did. She slid up and down his shaft, slow and easy, then hard and deep, until he filled her. When he tried to grasp her by the hips to quicken the pace, she pushed him back down and continued to sway her hips to her rhythm.

The shoe was certainly on the other foot now as she milked him, writhing her hips in one moment then kissing him long and hard in the next. He probed the inner sweetness of her mouth until he was gasping his need against her lips. "Baby, please," he groaned.

Only then did she increase her rhythm, moving quickly until she found exactly what pleased him. "Oh yes, baby, like that." He whispered words of encouragement until she took him on a journey unlike any he'd ever had. Their eyes locked at the exact moment that Angela reached her climax.

Still joined, Daniel gathered her in his arms and switched positions until Angela was underneath them. Then he began moving inside her again. He lost himself in her heat and she tightened her arms around him as he pounded even harder into her. She cried out just as his orgasm hit and his entire body shuddered. Then he collapsed on top of her.

Reaching for a throw on the opposite lounger, he tossed it over them and curled beside her on the lounger and closed his eyes.

Chapter 15

From the patio of the cottage, Angela stared out over the Gulf with a cup of coffee on Saturday morning. The sun had long since risen and Daniel was still sleeping, which gave her time to think. She was still grappling with how uninhibited she'd been with Daniel on the patio last night.

The kind of sex she'd shared with Daniel had made her feel closer to him than any other man she'd been with. She'd developed deep feelings, strong feelings, for this man. Feelings that resembled love. It was as if he'd captured something and now she felt like she belonged to him and vice versa. But she was unsure how Daniel felt because he kept his thoughts hidden.

Her only indication was how he responded in bed. He was open, honest and giving, but that was as far as it went. Sure, he treated her to the best and most luxurious things that life had to offer, but she suspected he did that with all his women. She'd worried about becoming one of them, a kept woman that he dangled beautiful, sparkly things in front of, but he'd surprised her with this getaway.

His choice was thoughtful and showed her he cared more about her comfort and wishes than his own. Wasn't that a thought she should hold on to?

She was wondering just that when she felt his strong, muscular arms encircle her waist and his lips nuzzle her neck.

"Good morning." He was bare-chested and she could feel his morning bulge in the boxer briefs he was wearing.

She gave him a sideward glance. "Good morning."

"How long have you been up?"

"Not long."

"I was hoping to persuade you to join me back in bed, but you're already dressed."

She was. She'd showered and changed into shorts and a halter top. She knew they were good in bed, but she wanted to see what more there was between them. "That's right. So what else do you have in store for the weekend?"

Daniel smiled. "I have a few ideas."

"Lay them on me," Angela said, leaving the patio and coming back indoors. She headed straight for the coffeepot to warm up her coffee. "Would you like a cup?" she asked, when she turned and found he'd followed her inside.

"Love one."

She poured him coffee into the mug she'd left sitting beside the pot and handed it to him. As he sipped, she watched him with avid interest. He looked as if he'd just walked off a *GQ* spread instead of standing there wearing only the briefs he'd slept in.

"If you're up for it and don't mind a little exercise, I thought we could bike up to Old Town, look at the nineteenth-century architecture, visit the Ernest Hemingway Home & Museum with its beautiful garden, then maybe trek our way up to the lighthouse and get a bird's-eye view of the entire island and then finish our hard work with a picnic lunch on the beach. How does that sound?"

Angela leaned across the countertop and felt Daniel's forehead with the back of her hand. "Are you feeling all right, because I could swear you're getting into playing tourist?"

He grinned. "Only because I'm with you," he responded. "You've never been before and I thought you might like to know some of the history. I saw you browsing through my collection of books at my penthouse the other day."

"Who would have known you were a closet history buff?"

"There's a lot you don't know about me," Daniel replied, cheekily. But as he said it, Angela knew it was true. They'd barely delved beneath the surface with each other. And it gave Angela pause. Should she continue down this path when the future was so uncertain?

"Angela," Daniel said, cutting into her thoughts. As if reading her mind he said, "Whatever you want to know, you can ask."

"Really?" She rubbed her chin. "Hmm… Let me think about it."

And for the next half hour, they did a speed round of getting to know each other. Angela learned he lost his virginity at sixteen with his eighteen-year-old neighbor in the back of his first car, a Nissan 200SX. She found out he hated cooking as much as she did, but equally enjoyed eating out. She also learned he hated brussels sprouts, but adored macaroni and cheese. His favorite movie was *Legends of the Fall* because Brad Pitt was an antihero and he liked his bravery in taking care of his brother. She even discovered that he was terribly afraid of frogs after an incident when one leaped into his mouth as a teenager, but generally loved all other animals.

What he was close-lipped about was his love life. When Angela asked if he'd ever been in love, he quickly changed the subject, rushing off into the shower to get ready for the day. She stared at his retreating form. She'd touched a nerve. And it made her wonder. Who was the woman who'd hurt him so badly that he kept women at arm's length?

Angela determined in that moment that he wouldn't do the same to her. Slowly but surely she'd work her way into his life and perhaps into his heart.

Daniel couldn't believe how much fun he was having with Angela. If anyone had told him that he'd break his cardinal rule and sleep with a coworker, he would have called them a bold-faced liar, but Angela wasn't just any woman. She was special. And the more time he spent with her, the more he was seeing how kind and caring she was.

He'd watched as she stopped her bike to help an old lady across the road as they made their way to Hemingway's house. And later he'd seen her explain the history of the lighthouse to a young girl who couldn't have been more than seven or eight years old. She had a natural, easy way with people that made them relax in her company, including him.

He would never have suggested this sort of date with any other woman he'd dated. They would have wanted to sit by the pool or be pampered in the spa, but not Angela. He loved seeing her blond-streaked waves blow in the wind as she let her hair down because he'd liked it that way. And he'd enjoyed seeing her tush hug on that bike. Several times, he'd wished she was riding him back at the cottage.

And she would later.

But for now, he would content himself with the time spent in her company. They were getting to know each other, and he hoped that their speed-dating session earlier at the house had helped alleviate some of her fears. He'd seen a strange look cross her face when he'd said she didn't know him.

And he didn't like it.

He wanted her happy, carefree and passionate when she was with him.

So he'd answered all her questions, everything from his favorite color and favorite food to the first time he'd had sex. He hadn't talked about his past relationships, especially because it was the one question he couldn't answer. Soon, the happy look he'd come to expect had returned to her face and they were back on track.

Now he was sitting across from her on the beach. They'd spread a large blanket on the sand so they could dive into the picnic basket they'd procured from a local delicatessen. Inside was a bottle of his favorite white wine, crusty bread, hard meats, cheeses, fruit and various salads. They nibbled, slicing sections from the bread, heaping them with meat and cheese and feeding each other.

Eventually, Angela had stripped off her shorts and halter top, revealing an itty-bitty bikini that showed way more skin than he would like the rest of the men on this beach to see. But he couldn't fault her; she had a beautiful body. He watched her bask in the sun and splash around in the water in front of him while he lounged on the blanket admiring her.

It didn't get any better than this, spending time with someone you loved.

Loved?

No, he didn't mean love. That was a figure of speech. He meant someone he enjoyed spending his time with. He didn't love anyone. Or would never again. Losing Mia at such a young age had had a profound effect on him. He'd learned that to get the girl, he would have to be smarter and richer than the next guy. He'd learned that nice guys finish last. He'd learned that if you wanted something in life you had to go for it, because tomorrow wasn't promised.

Look at what happened to Mia. Her life had been snuffed out in a flash and he was left with regrets. Should he have told her sooner of his feelings? Would that have made the difference? Perhaps she would never have looked in Ashton's direction. But he would never know. And when he'd been with Farrah, all he'd encountered was a wolf in sheep's clothing. Another woman looking for someone richer than him.

So he'd sworn off love. Put it on a shelf, because all it had ever given him was heartache.

It would be no different with Angela, because as much as he was starting to care for her, he didn't do long-term relationships. Theirs would have a beginning, a middle and an end.

Later, once the sun set, they made their way on bicycles back to the cottage and began one of the most sensual lovemaking sessions of his life.

It started first with Angela teasing him in the shower to wash off the sand, dirt and grime of the day. She'd taken the soap sponge and washed his chest and back before lowering herself to her knees. It wasn't the first time a woman had taken him in her mouth, and he usually kept his eyes shut, but he didn't this time. He watched her featherlight fingers kiss and stroke his fully aroused member. He watched the movement of her damp honey-blond tresses as her head bobbed up and down on him. Sweet Jesus! It was heaven. And he couldn't remember it ever feeling quite like…like…

Then he felt himself coming and to his delight she raised her head to look at him as she sucked him in—and it blew him away.

Eventually they finished showering and he scooped her in his arms and took her to the bedroom. He wanted full and unencumbered access to her. Her slick body slid onto the bed and he reached for the pack of condoms on the nightstand. After protecting them both, he flipped her over onto her stomach and entered her from behind.

She was so wet, Daniel thought he'd died and gone to heaven. He leaned over her to stroke and tweak her breasts with one hand, awakening her passion, while the other caressed her firm behind.

He wanted to possess her, ruin her for any other man. The thought sent shivers through him, and what had once been a slow yearning turned primal and he drove into her. She arched off the bed and met his every thrust. His body was aflame with desire, but he wanted her to come first, so he reached between them to tease her clitoris and Angela screamed as her orgasm struck. "Daniel!"

As she succumbed to her own orgasm, pleasure of the

purest kind hit him with such force that he cried out her name, "Angela!"

Afterward, their bodies melted together into one and they drifted off to sleep.

Chapter 16

Returning to the real world from their weekend of bliss wasn't an easy transition for Angela. She and Daniel had agreed to keep their relationship secret from the rest of the office. It meant Daniel, the darling of the gossip bloggers, had to keep a low profile. He'd welcomed the respite and had told Angela he wanted to be with her more than being in the public eye.

At work they maintained the same level of professionalism and decorum they had previously. For Angela it was difficult to spend so much time with him all day and keep her hands off him. But at night...

Oh, the nights were another matter entirely.

Once they got to his penthouse they came together and made sometimes sweet, sometimes hot passionate love into the wee hours of the morning, making it very difficult for Angela to rise for those early-morning showings.

A couple of weeks into their affair, Angela was feeling pretty good about her relationship with Daniel and about work. She'd landed her first sales offer for their new downtown development and was feeling so high, she didn't give a second thought to agreeing to dinner with her parents.

What harm could there be?

Later, Angela would regret her cavalier choice.

When she'd suggested taking her parents to their favorite restaurant, initially they'd balked, claiming it was too expensive, but eventually they'd acquiesced when she told them she'd landed a big contract.

Angela had just given the waiter their wine selection when her parents started in. She was becoming quite fluent in selecting wines, thanks to Daniel's impeccable taste.

"Two hundred dollars for a bottle of wine?" her father huffed. "Really, Angela, must you be so over the top?"

Angela rolled her eyes and prayed for patience. "I'm not being flashy, Dad. It happens to be an excellent vintage that *I* like. If you don't want any, don't drink it."

"Angela!" her mother cautioned.

"What?" She shrugged. She wasn't going to apologize for her good fortune any longer.

"Your father was just thinking of you. There's really no reason to go through all the trouble."

Angela released a long sigh. "It's no trouble, Mama. I *want* to do this. As I told you both earlier on the phone, I had clients put in a huge offer and it's a big coup for me."

"But you haven't actually sold it," her father stated. "Perhaps we should be celebrating *after* you've closed on the property."

"Don't rain on my parade, Daddy. Before joining Cobb Luxury Real Estate, I would never get clients of this caliber, but my career is on the upward swing now."

"Career?" Her mother chuckled. "C'mon, Angela. This is nothing more than another job you'll stay at for a few years before you move on to the next thing."

And then it came.

"I wish you were more like your sister, Denise," her mother continued. "Now that girl has her head on straight. She knows that the only way to get ahead is with a good education."

Angela reached for her wineglass. "You don't have to sing me Denise's praises," she responded, drinking her wine. "I've heard it all before."

"Then you would do well to listen," her father said.

"No, Daddy, you would do well to recognize the fact that I've finally found a career that I love, that I'm good at and that I make a good living at. It allows me to take you both out to fine meals such as this." She sipped her wine again. "Neither you nor Mama's principal salary ever afforded you this luxury."

"Don't you look down on your mama and me," her father reprimanded as he pointed his finger at her. "Education is a noble profession. We are helping today's youth. What are you doing? Helping rich people buy even richer real estate? How is that helping the world?"

"It actually stimulates the economy," Angela replied. "I believe I learned that in economics class."

Stunned, her father looked away, busying himself by tearing off a piece of bread and buttering it.

For once in her life, she'd finally silenced them. But why did she have to? She just wished her parents could support her half as much as they did Denise. She'd thought that today she'd finally lived up to the high ideals they'd set forth, but once again she was wrong.

When would she ever learn?

* * *

"Daniel," Ashton Rollins called out to him on his way into meeting with some prospective clients on Tuesday afternoon at his favorite restaurant in downtown Miami.

Daniel stopped midstride. He'd been hoping not to run into Ashton until after the coup was a fait accompli, but he hadn't heard from Joshua in a while and wondered how he was faring digging up dirt on their illustrious leader.

Daniel turned around and shook Ashton's hand. "What are you doing here?"

"Meeting my father and some of the board members of Rollins Aeronautics. We're discussing some products under development."

"Sounds promising."

Ashton shrugged. "Could be. Listen, do you have a few minutes? I'm a little early, so perhaps we could chat?"

Daniel didn't want to talk, but knew it would not only be rude, but would raise a red flag. "Sure, I have a few minutes before my clients arrive."

He joined Ashton at the bar. "Club soda," Daniel told the bartender.

"I'll have the same," Ashton responded before the bartender could ask.

"So, what's on your mind, Ashton?"

"Prescott George. And Joshua DeLong's influence."

"I don't follow."

"C'mon, Daniel." Ashton regarded him quizzically. "You and I both know that DeLong has it out for me. Has from the moment we let him into the club. I don't know why he has a beef with me. The only thing I can figure is it has something to do with my last name being on the wall."

The bartender placed both their club sodas on the bar,

and Daniel grasped his and took a swallow before replying, "You think a whole lot of yourself."

Ashton snorted. "I'm aware that some members of the organization think I live a privileged life, but it hasn't always been so." His eyes became guarded and something flashed in them that Daniel couldn't quite name. Guilt? Regret? Both? "You and I both know that."

"If you're talking about Mia, it's best not to go down that rabbit hole, Ashton."

"Why? We've never talked about her. She was important to both of us."

"No, she was in love with *you*," Daniel responded, tightly clutching his glass. The past was past. There was no rewriting history. Mia was dead, and no one or nothing was going to bring her back.

"You've always resented me for that," Ashton surmised correctly, "that she loved me and not you."

Daniel was surprised by the lack of malice in his tone. There had never been any love lost between the two men. Even when Ashton offered to bring him into Prescott George, they'd always had an uneasy alliance.

"Does it matter now?" Daniel inquired. "She's gone. And you're doing exactly what your father intended for you."

Ashton frowned. "That may be so, but I've never forgotten her, Daniel. We were going to get married, for Christ's sake. And I suspect neither have you. As a result, I always thought we had an odd sort of kinship because of that loss."

Daniel regarded him. That was a spin on the situation if ever there was one. He sipped his club soda. "What is it that you want from me, Ashton?" He turned to the matter at hand.

"I've heard rumblings," Ashton said. "Rumors that DeLong is coming after me. Is that true?"

"And if it were?"

"Do I have your support?"

Daniel stared him in the eye. "I won't lie to your face, Ashton. You have competition. And they've made a telling argument as to why I should vote their way."

Ashton stared at him warily. "Well, by your response, I guess I have my answer. It's good to know I can count on friends like you."

"We were never friends," Daniel said.

"Allies?" Ashton questioned.

"I suppose."

"And maybe we'll be again one day," Ashton responded. "For your sake as well as mine." His eyes darted to the door. "There's my father. I'll be talking to you."

And then he was gone, leaving Daniel feeling uneasy. He didn't like the direction their conversation had taken, and not just about Mia. Ashton seemed resigned to a fight between him and Joshua. Perhaps he wouldn't put up as much resistance as they'd initially thought? Was he, too, tired of the status quo? Or maybe Ashton was finally ready to come out from behind his father's shadow and walk his own path. And if so, what did that mean for the future of Millionaire Moguls?

Later that night, rather than reaching for Angela, who'd made it a habit of staying over at his penthouse over the last week, he was pensive in bed.

"Something on your mind?" Angela inquired.

"Hmm?" Daniel glanced up and found Angela standing by the bed wearing a very sexy negligee. "Babe... come over here."

"Oh no you don't." She patted his hand away as she slid under the covers and away from him. "I've been walking around in this nightie for the better part of a half hour and you've paid me no attention. Don't think you're going to get lucky now."

"Aaaw, c'mon." Daniel tried pulling her closer, but she resisted.

"Nope, it's been a long day for me, too, and if you don't want to talk about whatever is on your mind, that's fine. We can go to sleep." She reached for the lamp on the nightstand and turned it off, placing his bedroom in utter darkness.

"Angela," he crooned, wrapping his arms around her middle. "I'm sorry if I was preoccupied. I just have a lot on my mind."

"As do I," she responded, "but I engage with you. Instead, you shut down."

Daniel wasn't used to sharing his emotions with anyone, much less the women he was seeing. Usually they were in his life for one purpose—to fulfill his sexual needs. But Angela was quickly becoming more than just another roll in the hay. She was not just his lover, but she'd become his friend and apparently she wanted to be his confidant, as well.

"I'm sorry." He found himself apologizing. A first for him.

She kept her back to him.

He didn't want them to go to bed angry. He wanted her body to be wrapped around him as he slept so that he could awaken her sometime during the course of the night and make love to her. Then fall asleep again. It would be the best sleep elixir.

Still smarting over her parents' dismissal of her career the night before, Angela had been in a rotten mood all day. She'd hoped that seeing Daniel again after a night apart would soothe her ruffled feathers. Instead, he'd been distracted and distant.

She knew theirs wasn't a normal relationship, but was it too much to expect that if he didn't share his life with her he could at least share his day with her? Tell her about his upheavals? Apparently not. He only wanted her when it was convenient for him. She'd had a mind to get up and leave, but she was dog-tired from the day and from the evening class at Orangetheory. The interval fitness craze kept her fit and trim, but also kicked her behind. She'd been ready to unwind in Daniel's arms, but found he was less than interested in what she had to offer, even if it came wrapped up in the most expensive negligee she'd ever bought. The salesperson had sworn that once he saw her in it, she'd have the best night.

How wrong she'd been.

Eventually Angela drifted off to sleep, only to feel hot, chaste kisses on her neck. "Daniel, go back to sleep," she murmured.

But he wouldn't.

Instead she felt his hands massage her breasts through the negligee she wore.

"I'm sorry," he whispered. And this time, she felt his tongue inside her ear, swirling, nibbling and tasting.

She wanted to resist him, show him how upset she was, but her body betrayed her. And when he hauled her around to face him and she felt the weight of his mouth on hers, she gave in. Her lips parted…and then she felt his tongue, slipping slowly in and out, mingling, stroking her until she finally relaxed and accepted him. It was bliss, pure bliss, and she surrendered.

"I'm sorry," he said again, as he slowly trailed kisses

down her chest, brushing against her breasts as he made his way even lower.

Angela felt Daniel pushing her negligee up, and if she wasn't mistaken, she heard his sharp intake of breath at finding she wasn't wearing any panties. She was fully bare to his searing gaze, for him to do with as he would.

And he did.

Whispering "I'm sorry" one last time, he made his way to her most private place while his fingers pressed on her lips. She sucked them into her mouth greedily as he knew she would. Then his tongue was inside her, stroking her walls, teasing her clitoris. Tiny gasps escaped her throat as he worked his magic and lapped her up. The rhythmic feel of his tongue, hot, wet and thick, caused Angela to lose herself too quickly.

"Oh yes, oh yes…" she heard herself mutter as her climax came fierce and strong. She was still trembling and had yet to recover when she felt him at her entrance, felt the slippery heat of him slide effortlessly inside her, filling her.

It felt divine having him inside her. As he sped her toward another orgasm, Angela knew she was on the edge of losing herself to this man, and not just physically. She couldn't control or slow down her feelings any more than she could stop Daniel from moving in and out of her. She rose to meet his every thrust and he kissed her face, her neck, and she dug her fingers into his buttocks. And when ecstasy finally came, a million slivers of sublime pleasure spread through her and she sobbed out his name as she orgasmed. And in that moment, she realized how deeply she'd fallen in love with him.

Chapter 17

Daniel couldn't focus on work. How could he when Angela had responded to him this morning with utter abandon? Something had shifted between them. It had been subtle at first, but he could definitely tell that somehow without him knowing it, they'd fallen into a relationship.

In Key West, they'd talked about a carefree, casual relationship. That's what he'd thought he wanted. But now, when he wasn't with her, he missed her, and he found a way to ensure they never spent more than an evening apart. And at work under his eagle eye, Angela was blossoming. She'd already managed to get a signed offer for one of the units in the new development by the strength of her own contacts.

She was on her way. Daniel wondered what that might mean. Would she need him anymore? He dismissed the notion. She still had a long way to go before she made one-tenth of his earnings in a year, but he was definitely proud of her.

More than that, he wanted to celebrate her big sale, which they'd yet to do since she'd had dinner with her parents, then he'd been preoccupied and she'd gone to bed angry at him.

He smiled when he thought about how he'd woken her up and how good she'd tasted as she came all over his mouth.

"Daniel?"

He glanced up to find Myrna in the doorway. "Yes, Myrna?"

"Several of us in the office were going to take Angela out to celebrate her big sale. You interested in coming?"

Daniel thought about it. He didn't want the appearance of impropriety between them to hurt Angela at the agency. He was sure they'd already sparked some gossip when they'd both been absent on the same day, so he didn't want to add any more fuel to the fire. He was still her boss. "You all go ahead."

He would celebrate with her later. In private.

Angela anxiously tapped her feet at the reception desk while she waited with several of the other agents for Myrna to return. She couldn't wait to spend some time with Daniel. After the revelation of her feelings last night, she was admittedly nervous, yet excited to see him.

So when Myrna rounded the corner without Daniel, her heart sank, but she plastered a plastic smile on her face anyway.

"Boss is too busy," Myrna said.

"Of course," Angela responded. "Let's go, then."

Throughout the lunch, Angela accepted praise and

congratulations from her peers, but that's not who she wanted them from. She wanted Daniel's presence and *his* acceptance of her and how she was blossoming under his tutelage, but he was "too busy" to give her notice. She doubted that was the truth. Had he somehow guessed that her feelings for him had changed from lust to love? Did he need to let her down easy?

The look of worry on her face when she should have been celebrating caused Myrna to say, "For someone who just landed the biggest sale of their career, you sure don't look happy."

Angela laughed nervously. "Oh, you know how it is," she responded. "Once I sell one, now I gotta keep right on selling."

She knew her response was feeble at best, but she had to save face. She didn't want Myrna to call her out. Hadn't the young woman already warned her that Daniel never kept a woman for long? Why should she be any different?

When they returned to the office, Angela created a fake appointment so she could use the remainder of the afternoon for some much-needed retail therapy. She wasn't upset with Daniel; she just needed to get her head back on straight. She couldn't blame him if he didn't feel the same way about her. She supposed she'd just been hoping against hope that he would fall for her as she had him.

By 6:00 p.m., she returned to her apartment having bought two new pair of shoes. A fierce pair of pumps from Alexander McQueen and a rocking pair of sexy sandals from Jimmy Choo. They'd cost her nearly a thousand dollars, but thanks to the hefty commission she would make on the development sale, Angela felt like she could splurge a little.

After showering, she decided to take a walk in her fabulous Jimmy Choos around her apartment. Turning on her iPod on the docking station, she was prancing around her apartment wearing a T-shirt and nothing but her heels when the doorbell rang.

Angela glanced down at her watch. She wasn't expecting any takeout. She sashayed over to the door and glanced through the peephole.

It was Daniel.

"Angela, I can hear you on the other side," he said from the doorway. "Let me in."

She glanced in the mirror near her door. Her hair was piled high on her head in a messy bun, and she had on an old college T-shirt. She was far from the sex kitten he was used to.

"Give me a minute," she yelled back.

"That's ridiculous. I know how you look naked. Open up." He knocked loudly on the door.

Well, if he didn't want to give her time to get jazzed up, then it was his own fault. Better he see that she wasn't glamorous like his other women every moment of every single day. Unlatching the door, Angela swung it open with a whoosh just as Daniel's hand was about to knock again.

Daniel grinned when he saw Angela. She was wearing a ratty old T-shirt that had seen better days and barely reached her thighs, showing him and whoever was behind him an indecent amount of leg. And the sexiest heels he'd seen her in yet. Quickly, he shut the door, but not before he reached behind him to pick up the flowers and large box he'd brought with him to celebrate.

"Love what you're wearing."

She chuckled. "Sure you do." And she turned to walk into the living room, not even glancing behind her to see him bring in the gifts. "I bet all those glam women you date wear heels and a T-shirt."

"Not quite like you do." Daniel appreciated the hint of her backside as he followed her into the room. "And as for this," he said as he motioned to the tuxedo he was wearing, "there is an explanation."

"Oh yeah, what's that?" she asked, turning around.

He offered her the roses. "Congratulations." He leaned forward to kiss her lips, but got her cheek instead.

She smiled halfheartedly. "Thank you. These are lovely." She took them into the kitchen and he watched her place them in a vase. "But I have to admit I'm surprised to see you. What are you doing here? Did we have plans? You don't usually like to come to my place."

"Whoa, whoa, whoa!" Daniel fanned his hands up and down. "Slow down. Can't I surprise the woman I'm seeing?"

She paused for just a moment longer than he would have liked before saying, "Of course."

He released a heavy sigh. "I was hoping we could celebrate. I've come to take you out to dinner."

"So we can celebrate. Just the two of us?"

He nodded. "Yes, is that a problem?"

She shook her head, and some of her hair spilled out from the messy bun atop her head. He liked her like this. Easy and carefree like she'd been in Key West when the subterfuge between them wasn't necessary. When they didn't have to worry about gossips and bloggers snapping a picture of them and posting it on social media. But the place he'd thought of to take her tonight was perfect.

"Here." He handed her the large white box he'd come in with.

"What is it?"

"Open it."

She raised a brow, but did as instructed. He watched her expression turn from wariness to awe as she lifted the designer gown from the tissue paper. "Daniel?" She peered at him. "What have you done?"

"We're celebrating in style. Now go change. A celebration awaits you."

"What? I look a wreck. I need more time."

"You have half an hour."

He was duly impressed with her efforts when she emerged from her bedroom on time wearing the floor-length beaded bronze gown with a side slit that reached her thigh. With her hair flowing in loose waves down her svelte back, she looked like a golden goddess.

"You're breathtaking," he said as she walked toward him.

She smiled. "It's the dress."

He shook his head. "No, it's most definitely the woman."

Five minutes later, they were seated in the limo he had waiting downstairs to whisk them away to the Vizcaya Museum & Gardens. He'd rented the place out for the night, so he could have a romantic candlelit dinner for two along the water's edge.

Daniel could only hope Angela liked the surprise, since he'd sensed she hadn't been happy with his failure to join their colleagues earlier.

"So where are we going?" Angela inquired.

"You'll see." Daniel reached for one of her hands and gave it a gentle squeeze. When she tried to pull away, he didn't let her go. He didn't know why but he wanted—no, *needed*—to feel connected. He didn't want the distance between them he'd felt when he'd entered her apartment. She hadn't even greeted him with her usual kiss and hadn't kissed him even after he'd given her the one-of-a-kind dress. If he was honest, he missed her lips on his. The feel of them brushing against his mouth was the highlight of his day.

After the short drive, Daniel exited the limo first and reached for Angela's hand to help her out. When she disembarked, she smiled warmly as she recognized the venue. "Daniel Cobb, you continue to surprise me. You do listen."

"Yes, I do."

They'd talked about the Vizcaya Museum and its beautiful gardens when they'd been in Key West. He remembered Angela mentioning it was one her favorite spots. The idea had come to him then that one day, he'd shut it down for her, for the two of them to share.

He offered his arm and she took it willingly.

"This is lovely," she said as he reached for her hand and led her into the museum. The curator was waiting for him.

"Mr. Cobb, so lovely to have you and your guest join us this evening."

"It's truly a pleasure to be here."

"Select areas of the museum are available to you for an hour before dinner service is set to begin."

Daniel nodded. "Thank you."

They strolled through the highlighted areas the curator had kept open, like the living room with its many artifacts from the Renaissance to the music room with its lush wall canvases. Eventually they made it to the loggia. "It was said this is where James Deering, the industrialist who built this home, had his guests relax and view the gardens. Would you care to walk them?" Daniel asked.

"So formal, Mr. Cobb." Angela laughed but went along with his attempt at romance. "I would love to."

They walked hand in hand through the formal European gardens. Dusk had long since gone and all they had was the soft ground lighting and moonlight to illuminate their view. Eventually, they walked toward the Tea House, guided by a lighted walkway. It had to be one of the most romantic settings he'd ever arranged, but Daniel sensed Angela was guarded tonight. And he didn't like it.

Finally when he could take it no longer, he stopped inside the open-air room. Angela was staring up at the dome as if it were the most interesting piece of architecture, when he knew she'd seen it countless times. "Please don't be angry with me anymore. I can't take your silence."

"Silence? We've been talking for the last hour."

"Like strangers about art and history. You're not your usual bubbly self."

She frowned. "Well, I'm not sure what you want, Daniel. There are so many rules. When we're at work, we can't associate with each other. When we're together, we can't be seen in public. So pardon me if I'm not sure how to behave on any given occasion. Perhaps you should tell me?"

Daniel sucked in a deep breath. This romantic date wasn't going as he envisioned. He was trying his best to show Angela how important she was to him within the boundaries he could live with.

He rushed toward her and hauled her against him. There was little doubt she could feel how hard he was, because that's how she made him whenever she was near.

He heard her sharp intake of breath seconds before his head descended. He brushed his mouth against hers, and an instant shimmer of lust surged through him.

He looked in her eyes when she pushed him away. "Sex is your answer for everything, isn't it?"

"No, it's not," Daniel replied, "but you know how I feel about you, Angela, that I enjoy spending time with you."

"Just not with other people around. I get it, okay? I agreed to a secret affair," Angela replied, jerking away from him and walking over to look out over the dark water. "Putting it into practice has been harder than I anticipated."

Daniel's hands came to her shoulders. "Let me make it up to you. I have a beautiful dinner planned for you tonight. Can we please enjoy it?"

She spun around to face him and he held out his hand to her. He knew full well that the conversation between them was far from over, but he was trying to salvage the night. "Please."

She nodded. "All right."

Dinner was on the stamped concrete on the East Terrace overlooking Biscayne Bay, and Angela had to admit that Daniel had gone to great lengths to impress her tonight. Perhaps to make up for his embarrassing faux pas earlier at the office when he'd treated her like a leper?

"Did you know this outdoor space was originally considered to be the front of the house," Angela inquired, "where small boats came to dock?"

"No, I didn't know that."

She shrugged. "Just little facts that I know."

"You're a wealth of knowledge and a talented real estate agent," Daniel offered. "I know it and so does everyone at the office. It's one of the reasons they came to your lunch today—to check out the competition."

"You think so?"

"Oh, I know it," he replied, "because it's the same thing I would do."

They continued talking over dinner, and slowly Angela began to relax and enjoy herself. Daniel had been right. At the start of the night she had been admittedly miffed by his behavior at the office, but she had only herself to blame. Daniel was a man who could compartmentalize his feelings. Work in one box. Angela in another. Millionaire Moguls in another.

It wasn't so easy for Angela to separate her life. For her the boxes took on different shapes and sizes and melded together. She was trying to make sense of where she fit in Daniel's world and whether she would be happy solely in the one box. For Angela, it had always been important to color outside the lines. Be her own person. It was part of her individuality.

Would staying with Daniel limit her in ways she wasn't willing to compromise?

Dessert came nearly an hour later and Angela didn't have the appetite to indulge in the three-chocolate soufflé because she was upset over Daniel's actions earlier at the office. She picked at it until eventually the waiter came to take it away.

Just when she thought the evening was over, a saxophonist came down the steps of the terrace and began playing Kenny G's "Forever in Love."

"Would you care to dance?" Daniel asked, rising to his feet and extending his hand.

Angela scooted her chair back. "Would love to."

When Daniel pulled her into his arms, all ideas of how

wrong things were between them flew out of her head, leaving Angela with only one thought. How good they were together and how great it felt to be in his arms. She knew it was crazy to wish for something that might never be, but maybe no other woman had tried to win Daniel's heart before. And maybe she could.

She glanced up at him and when she did, she got lost in his dark eyes. Eyes that seemed to look into her very soul. And when he lowered his head to kiss her, she didn't pull away, because she loved him. Instead, she circled her arms around his neck and drew him in.

"Ready to go home?" he whispered when they both pulled away, breathless and greedy with desire.

She nodded.

In the limo on the short ride back to her place, they were both quiet in their own thoughts. But once they reached the door to her apartment, there was no thought of talking, only action. They were hungry for each other as they stepped out of their shoes and began tearing at each other's clothes. A trail of apparel, including her designer dress, was left from her living room floor to her bedroom in their quest to be naked.

They sank inexorably into each other on the bed, kissing with such unstoppable desire it left Angela feeling weak and dizzy. She could feel every taut muscle of his rock-hard body imprinted against her, and she couldn't resist splaying her fingers possessively over his back. He was hers for now and that's all that mattered. She watched him roll on a condom. Then he positioned himself, braced on his forearms and entered her. The sensation was slow, but felt so right, and when he lifted her bottom and went deeper she arched her hips, pulling him in to the hilt.

Angela felt powerful and she knew that no matter how

it ended with Daniel, she would be open and vulnerable and give of herself as she'd never done before. As Daniel moved, an ache began to build inside her with such force, she felt like she might explode. She writhed her hips in rhythm with his and clutched his shoulders as sensations overwhelmed her. They both reached their peak at the same time, exploding with pleasure and crying out as one.

Chapter 18

Daniel was happy that his relationship with Angela returned to normal during the subsequent week, or as least how it had been after Key West. They shared the occasional showing together during the workday, but at night they came together harmoniously in bed. Her responses to him were completely open and unfettered. She was so selfless in the giving of her body that Daniel was beginning to wonder if this was what love felt like.

If so, it scared him. He'd thought he was in love with Mia and look how that ended. And then there'd been Farrah. He wasn't sure he even knew what love was and if he'd recognize it. Love complicated things, and he led an uncomplicated life.

Or so he thought. Angela had made his life warm and inviting. With her, his life played out in vivid color while before he'd felt as if he lived only in black and white. She may not have thought he paid attention, but he'd seen her feminine touches around the house: fresh flowers in his kitchen, a framed photograph of the two of them in Key West on his shelf and her toothbrush next to his in the bathroom.

He'd never had to share his space with another woman because their presence in his life had always been temporary, but he'd never enjoyed any other woman's company as much as Angela's. However, he did have reservations. Would she begin to dream of a happy future with him, with marriage and the proverbial white picket fence? He would hate to shatter her world, but he wasn't sure that it was in the cards for him. Though he had to admit she was the first woman to make him think along those lines.

He needed to talk to someone about his trepidations and it so happened that Joshua called him to talk about Millionaire Moguls, presenting him with just the outlet.

A week later, Daniel met Joshua at a waterside open-air bar near Brickell Key. They sat down to enjoy drinks and cigars and to talk strategy.

"I've been able to bring a few more members over to our side," Joshua commented after their drinks were ordered, "but not nearly enough if we want to overthrow Ashton."

Daniel chuckled. "You act like we're taking over a monarchy or something."

Joshua laughed, as well. "I guess that was a bit dramatic, but the Rollinses have been an institution and it won't be easy ousting the favorite son."

"There's going to be fallout, no doubt," Daniel said, "but as long as we have the majority of members on our side, it stands to reason that we will prevail."

"You're sounding very upbeat," Joshua said. "Considering how helpful the Rollinses have been to you in opening doors to the elite."

"They may have opened the door to some folks I may not have met initially on my own, but I've grown my business with my expertise and business acumen. Speaking of the Rollinses, I saw Ashton recently."

"Oh yeah? What happened?"

"He knows you're coming for him."

Joshua shrugged. "Good. It's good to know he's got a little bit of paranoia where I'm concerned."

"You're not nervous that he could waylay our plans?"

"No." Joshua shook his head. "Because I'm right." At Daniel's frown, he amended, "*We're* right. Millionaire Moguls needs fresh blood, and once everyone hears our new ideas, they'll believe it, too."

"Cheers to that." Daniel held up his scotch and Joshua his beer.

"So, what else is new with you? How's that pretty agent you brought with you a while back?"

"Angela?"

Joshua grinned. "Of course, Angela. You couldn't take your eyes off her the entire night."

Daniel nodded. He hadn't been able to since, which was his problem. "True. And our relationship has progressed since then."

"Progressed?" Joshua inquired. "So you're an item?"

"I wouldn't call it that," Daniel stated, "but we have been seeing quite a bit of each other."

"And that's making you nervous?" Joshua quickly surmised.

Daniel turned to stare at him. "Is it that obvious?" Did he have *commitment-phobe* written on his forehead?

Joshua threw back his head and laughed. "Yeah, there's a little bit of fear on your mug."

Daniel sat forward in his seat. "I don't know what it is. I really enjoy her company... It's just things are moving quickly, too quickly for my liking."

"How so?"

"We've kind of settled into an easy habit of her sleeping over and I like it, but there's things starting to pop up all over the place. Today, it's a toothbrush, tomorrow she'll want a drawer, then a key..."

"Then marriage?" Joshua added, verbalizing Daniel's fears.

"I don't want to give her the wrong impression that this is anything other than a good time. I'm starting to feel a bit suffocated."

"Have you had that conversation with her?"

Daniel nodded. "I thought I had. I mean, we discussed that we were going to keep our relationship on the down low, given that she works for me, so I guess I just assumed that the parameters were understood."

Joshua snorted. "Make no assumptions where women are concerned, Daniel. You need to be straight up and honest with Angela about your intentions—or lack thereof."

Daniel was quiet as he mused over that notion before finally speaking. "I don't know how she's going to take it. What if she walks away?"

"That's the million-dollar question, right?" Joshua asked, sipping his drink. "You're going to have to figure out just how important she is to you and if your independence is worth the risk of losing her."

Daniel nodded his agreement. Joshua was right. He and Angela needed to discuss where their relationship was headed. He wanted breathing room, but he also didn't want to lose what they shared. How did he share with Angela how he was feeling without losing her?

"Can you zip me up?" Angela asked Daniel as he stood admiring her from the doorway of her apartment on Saturday night. She was wearing a black leather minidress with a cutout back while he was dressed in all black. They were on their way out for a night on the town. Daniel had promised her they'd go dancing for some time and was finally making good on that promise. She'd made sure to pack an overnight bag because they would spend the night back at his penthouse.

"Of course." He rose from his seat and stepped behind her.

Their eyes met in the mirror and the heat in them caused Angela's heart to speed up. He slowly zipped up the dress, never taking his eyes off her.

"You look great," he murmured huskily, and bent his head to kiss her shoulder.

She smiled. "Thank you." She spun around to face him and he circled his arms around her waist. "So are you ready to show me all your moves?"

He pulled her closer to him until she was pressed against his groin. "You know most of my moves, but there are a few I haven't shown you yet."

Angela laughed. "You're a flirt."

"And you love it."

Angela bit back a retort. She did love his flirting as much as she loved the man. But she couldn't say that. If she did, Daniel would run in the other direction. "Let's go." She slapped him on the bottom and slid out of his hands before he could retaliate.

Shortly thereafter, they were seated in the VIP area of a popular nightclub as the strobe lights and music pulsed around them. "This place is great," Angela said very loudly. She wasn't at all surprised Daniel opted for bottle service in lieu of being in the throng below them on the first floor. The plush leather sofas were certainly pleasant enough.

Angela, however, intended to pull Daniel from his comfort zone and dance with the crowd downstairs. She loved that he treated her like a queen and showed her how much he cared by his actions, but it wouldn't hurt him to verbalize them. Dancing would be a way for him to speak to her without saying the words.

"To a great night," Daniel said once the waitress had returned with a bottle of Cristal and handed them each flutes.

"Cheers." Angela tapped her flute with his. Daniel leaned back on the sofa while she sat forward and tapped her foot in time to the music as she looked below. She was dying to get out there.

When a particularly good song came on, she couldn't resist rising to her feet and placing the flute on the cocktail table in front of her. She held out her hand. "Let's go downstairs and dance."

Daniel regarded her. "What's wrong with dancing right here? It's less noisy and far less crowded."

"But not nearly as much fun," she said, giving him a wink. She inclined her head. "Let's go."

Reluctantly, Daniel rose to his feet. "All right." He took her hand and together they went down the stairs.

Once they were in the crowd, Daniel pushed his way through the throng to carve out a small area for them. Then he stepped forward and moved in on her, wrapping his hands around her hips. "That's better," he whispered in her ear.

The deep rumble of his throat sent a flood of warmth spreading through Angela's body. That's the effect Daniel had on her whenever she was around him. Just the sound of his voice made her want him in some primitive way.

His hands were hot and possessive on her bare back thanks to the dress she wore, but she did her best to match his moves. They swayed together and it was clear Daniel was a great dancer. Angela found herself excited and exhilarated.

There was a wicked glint in her eye when they pulled apart and performed a sexy sashay around each other. "You're good," Daniel commented.

"Are you surprised?"

"Not at all. You're good at everything you set your mind to."

She whirled around him and worked off a quick set of dance moves until her backside came up to his groin. She moved her body sensuously up and down his body, and when he could take no more, his hands drew her up by her shoulders. "You keep doing that, you're going to have me take you right here on the dance floor," he said huskily.

She spun around to face him. "I might like that."

He chuckled, then grabbed her by the hand and led her off the dance floor. They were walking up the stairs when a stunningly gorgeous woman stopped in front of them. She was wearing a glittery halter top and a skirt that stopped well above her thighs.

"Daniel."

Angela instantly stiffened at her use of his first name. The woman knew him. Intimately. She could see it by the glare the other woman gave her as she eyed Angela up and down.

"Farrah."

Who was this woman, Angela wondered, and what did she mean to him?

"Aren't you going to introduce me to your companion?" the woman asked, all pouty red lips, smoky eyes and flawless skin.

Angela disliked her on the spot.

"Farrah, Angela. Angela, this is Farrah."

Farrah extended her hand, but Angela declined to shake it. She wasn't going to attempt social graces when it was clear the other woman didn't like her.

"Well…" Farrah huffed. "I'm sure I'll be seeing you again, Daniel." She glared at Angela before leaving.

Once they were sitting back in VIP, Daniel said, "I'm sorry about that."

Angela shrugged. "No worries. We both have a past. If you'll excuse me for a moment, I'm going to go freshen up." In actuality, she needed a breather to settle her nerves. Angela didn't know what it was, but something about that woman told her she and Daniel had a shared history that went deeper than just a sexual relationship.

There was something in Farrah's eyes that told Angela she knew something Angela didn't. Was there a note of pity there?

She got her answer several moments later. She was in the ladies' room and had just freshened up her lipstick when Farrah entered.

Farrah gave a dry chuckle. "If it isn't Daniel's new woman of the week. Or is it a month?" She laughed at her own joke.

Angela didn't respond and instead pulled out her comb

to freshen her look after being on the dance floor. "If you have something to say, you might as well spit it out."

Farrah took a step backward and regarded her in the mirror. "Well, someone's pretty sure of herself. That's surprising considering you're with Mr. No Commitment himself, Daniel Cobb. I'm sure he's taking you to nice places, buying you fancy things, but in the end, if you're looking for more, it'll never go any further than that."

Angela spun around to face her. "I know who Daniel is."

"Do you? Or do you know what he wants you to know?" Farrah responded. "Because I doubt you know the full story."

"No? Enlighten me, then." Angela hoped she wouldn't regret those words.

Farrah laughed. "It's your funeral," she replied. "If you don't know that Daniel hasn't gotten over his dead girlfriend, his one and only true love, then you're the one who's deluded. You will always live in the shadows of the great Mia Landers because no one, including me, can compete against a ghost. But hey, if you think you're up to the challenge, knock yourself out. Others of us have tried and failed miserably."

Farrah gave one final toss of her curls and then strode out of the ladies' room, leaving Angela stunned in her wake and staring at the door.

Who the hell was Mia? And why was she hearing about her from Farrah and not Daniel?

Daniel didn't like the look on Angela's face when she returned. "Everything all right?" He stared at her, trying to assess her mood.

She sighed deeply. "Everything's fine. I just have a

headache is all. Do you mind if we leave and call it an early night?"

He shook his head. "Of course not. C'mon," he said as he wrapped his arm around her shoulder. "I'll take you home."

As they walked down the stairs, he caught sight of Farrah perched at a stool near the bar. Daniel didn't like the triumphant look on her face, as if she'd scored a direct hit. Was she the reason Angela was feigning a headache?

Angela had been perfectly fine before when it had just been the two of them in VIP and then on the dance floor. In fact, she'd been the most saucy he'd ever seen her. The way she'd swayed her curvy behind against his manhood, he'd gotten an instant erection and had been happy to escape back upstairs. But then they'd seen Farrah and *something* had transpired between the two women. He didn't know what it was, but he was determined to find out.

The driver came around to pick them up in the town car he'd hired for the night. Daniel helped Angela inside and slid in beside her. She was silent for most of the ride home to his place, resting her head on his shoulder. Once they made it inside the penthouse, Angela immediately went into the bathroom. Meanwhile Daniel went to his wet bar to make himself a drink. He didn't know what happened between Farrah and Angela.

Daniel walked out on the balcony and looked up at the darkened night sky. Had Farrah said something to upset her? Farrah could certainly be catty when cornered, but Angela was working off a deficit. He'd never mentioned Farrah when they'd briefly discussed past relationships. He just hoped Farrah hadn't shared his past with Angela. She was the only woman he'd ever opened up to about Mia and she'd used it against him, telling him she wouldn't be compared to a dead woman. Had she shared that same concern with Angela? Was that why Angela was suddenly so distant?

He had to know. He downed his drink and went inside to find Angela. When he made it to the bedroom, she was already in bed.

A first.

She usually waited up for him.

He frowned, but didn't say anything. Instead he went over to his side of the bed and began to undress. Toeing off his shoes, he unbuckled his belt and eased his pants down. His shirt soon followed and he laid them across the end of the bed. When he went to slide in beside her, his mood brightened a bit upon finding her nude underneath the sheets. The fact that she hadn't put clothes between them told him she was not closed off to him.

"You okay?" he asked, pulling her into his arms. He was happy when she didn't resist and allowed him to hold her.

She nodded. "Guess the music got the better of me."

He doubted it was true. He suspected Farrah was the cause of the abrupt end to their evening. What could he do to make it right?

He knew only one way. And so he began to touch her with featherlight caresses and to drop kisses across her lips, cheeks, eyes. She didn't stop him when he continued his exploration by lashing his tongue across her breasts. He knew she liked it when he grazed his teeth across the soft swells, so he pleased her and himself by tugging one nipple into his mouth and sucking it.

She moaned softly, but didn't say a word. Instead, she allowed him to kiss and lick her into a sweet torment. First her breasts, then lower to her abdomen, and lower still until his fingers parted the moist folds of her sex. He teased with slow, tantalizing strokes until he felt her muscles tense. He didn't want her to come yet; he wanted to be inside her when that happened.

Rolling over, he reached for the drawer on his nightstand. After putting on protection, he surged forward and drove himself into her.

"Daniel!" she cried out his name.

"I've got you," Daniel said as he grasped her hips and then kissed her hard, awakening the passionate nature in her.

She responded and began to rock to his rhythm as he moved inside her. He took them both to the pinnacle of ecstasy, marveling in the fact that only Angela made him feel this way, so complete and so whole. They reached a glorious climax and Daniel shouted as bliss pulsed through him. He hugged her close afterward, wanting in that moment to stay joined with her forever.

Chapter 19

Angela stared blankly at the computer screen in front of her on Monday morning. She'd been trying unsuccessfully to put together a launch for a new listing Daniel wanted her to work on, but her mind wasn't on it.

Ever since meeting Daniel's ex-girlfriend at the nightclub, she'd been distracted. Distracted by Farrah's words. And her predictions.

Was Farrah right?

She knew Daniel's reputation, but she'd always thought it was because he didn't know love or hadn't seen it to recognize what might be staring him in the face. Instead, she was faced with the knowledge that perhaps he *had* already seen it—when he was younger. And now he'd found every woman since Mia Landers lacking.

Oh how she wished Daniel had shared this information with her himself. Wished she hadn't heard this news from Farrah, but she had. And there was no going back. She had to know the truth.

Clicking on her mouse, Angela finally did what she'd been wanting to do since yesterday. She researched Mia Landers.

Ten minutes later, Angela was confused. According to what she read online, Mia Landers had been engaged to Ashton Rollins when she'd died in a car crash. Where did Daniel fit in? Had Mia left him for Ashton? Or had she been cheating on Ashton with Daniel? Angela didn't understand.

It didn't make sense.

Why would Daniel still carry a torch for another man's fiancée?

And did she have the guts to ask him about it in person? Angela rose from her chair and paced her office. She hadn't asked for this information, but now that it had been laid at her feet, she was curious. What did it all mean? And how did it affect her relationship with Daniel?

Only Daniel could answer these questions. And she had to know the truth. She was just afraid of rocking the boat. Everything was going so well between them. If she brought up his past, a past that he'd chosen not to share with her, would he consider it an invasion of his privacy?

Before she blew up a promising relationship, she would take some time to think about it. Another day wouldn't hurt…

Daniel was irritated. He'd arrived home later that evening with his dry cleaning and went to put it away only to find some of Angela's clothes hanging up in his closet.

Had he told her she could make herself at home? She hadn't even asked him. Perhaps if she had, he wouldn't feel like the walls were caving in on him, but he did.

He hated that he felt this way.

Angela was a good woman, but their relationship was moving at a galloping rate. He just wished he could slow it down so he could catch his breath and figure out what was going on. Before long, she would be moving in, and he wasn't sure if he was ready for it.

He hadn't even gotten this far with Farrah because he'd made sure to keep their two worlds separate. The only reason Farrah had even known about Mia was because an old college buddy had mentioned her name during a dinner, forcing him to discuss her. Daniel sure as hell wouldn't have confided in Farrah otherwise. He'd kept his feelings for Mia to himself. It was one of his greatest failures, and he wasn't happy to reveal them to anyone.

But Angela... She was changing everything. She was getting under his skin and slowly burrowing her way into his heart. He wasn't sure he could deal with putting himself out there again and risk losing his heart. He'd kept his heart shuttered for so long, he had to protect himself.

So when Angela came over later that night, he did what he did best. He turned the tables.

"Hey, babe." Angela's lips brushed his cheek as she walked past him carrying several plastic bags to the kitchen counter. "Hope you're hungry and don't mind Italian. I brought takeout from Mariano's."

"That's fine." He closed the door behind her and followed her into the kitchen. He sat on one of the stools in front of the island.

"How was your day?" she asked, removing the jacket that matched her suit. She was wearing a simple Dior pantsuit and looked sophisticated and sexy, and Daniel's heart turned over in his chest.

This woman was starting to make him feel something he

wasn't sure he was ready to face. When they were together in each other's arms, he wanted to stay with her forever.

He couldn't breathe.

He loosened his tie around his collar, desperate for air.

When he didn't answer, she glanced in his direction. "Daniel? Did you hear me?"

"Yes, I heard you," he replied tightly. "My day was fine."

She frowned at him. "The second 'fine' in a couple of minutes. It doesn't sound like your day went very well." She stopped unpacking the foil tins from the bag, moved away from the island and came toward him. Before he could stop her, she walked between his legs and slid her arms around his neck. "I'm sorry if you had a bad day. Is there anything I can do to help?"

She lowered her head to nuzzle his neck.

Daniel shook his head. "Just a lot on my mind, preoccupied with work." He pushed her away from him. He couldn't think with her hot lips on him.

She stared at him, looking into his eyes, and he knew she knew he was lying. "No, that isn't all, is it?"

He pushed off from the stool. "Just let it go, Angela."

She frowned, folding her arms across her chest. "Is it me? Have I done something to upset you?"

"No. Can't we just drop it?" He walked to the cupboard and began removing plates. "Let's just eat dinner."

Angela placed her hands on her hips. "I couldn't care less about dinner, Daniel. I'd like to know what it is I've done since I've only just arrived."

"You left your clothes in my closet!" Daniel said in a rush.

The moment he said the words and saw the subsequent hurt look on her face, Daniel instantly regretted it and wished he could take it back, but it was too late.

"Oh, I see." Angela's voice was shaky as she responded. "You don't mind having sex with me any day of the week, but heaven forbid I leave a change of clothes in your closet. Is that what you're telling me, Daniel?"

"Don't put words in my mouth."

She glared at him. "I don't need to." She stalked up the stairs to his bedroom and Daniel rushed to follow her. He knew what she was about to do and he was right. When he arrived, he found her in his closet snatching her clothes off the hangers and stuffing them in a bag. He stepped in her path, but she merely brushed past him and stormed into the master bathroom, taking her toothbrush from the holder next to his and throwing it in the bag.

"Angela, wait," he said as she stalked out of the bedroom and rushed down the stairs.

He watched her eyes dart around his penthouse and when she found her iPad on the settee next to the couch, she threw it in the bag.

"Angela, stop. You don't have to do this."

She stood still and glared at him. "Of course I do, Daniel, because I wouldn't want to crowd you. You're used to your bachelor lifestyle where women are interchangeable, and I've crossed the line."

"You're overreacting," Daniel said. "And I'm sorry if I've made you feel unwelcome. That wasn't my intention. You know I enjoy your company and I've always treated you well, haven't I? You've been happy with me?"

Angela laughed. "Of course, Daniel, you know I have. It's been nothing but the best Miami has to offer, but there is more to life than fancy dinners, private jets, beachside cottages and front-row seats at Heat games."

Daniel glanced at her warily. Where the hell had that come from? "You've never complained before."

"And I'm not now, Daniel. You've been nothing but generous. What's not to like?"

He heard the sarcastic note in her tone and ignored it. "Then why are you angry at me? Because I was just being honest. Our relationship is moving at an alarming rate and I hadn't realized we were at the stage of leaving our belongings at each other's place. We haven't talked about where this is leading. What exactly are you looking for?"

Was now the time to tell Daniel how she truly felt? If she didn't, Angela would never get another chance. She had to be completely honest with herself and him about what she wanted—no matter the consequences. Even if it meant losing him. Because hadn't she already?

Dropping her bag to her floor, Angela turned to face him. "Well, it's not what you think, Daniel. You can relax. I don't need a ring on my finger or a Mrs. before my name."

She couldn't read his expression. Was it a look of relief or disappointment on his face that she wasn't ready to throw herself headlong into marriage? Angela wasn't sure.

"What do you need?" Daniel queried.

"I need," Angela responded softly, "*all* of you."

"You have all of me. What you see is what you get, Angela. I'm not hiding anything from you."

"C'mon, Daniel," she said on a sigh. "You share only what you want me to see, what you share with the rest of the world—a perfectly polished Daniel Cobb with your shiny glass penthouse and your well-ordered life. And what have I brought into it? Chaos. I've interrupted your carefully constructed life. Well, guess what, I think there's more to you than this." She swept her arm around the room. "And I want that, Daniel. I want the full, unvarnished, unedited Daniel Cobb."

His brown eyes darkened as he held her gaze. "I'm not hiding anything."

A painful knot formed in her stomach, but she asked the question she'd wondered about since her encounter with Farrah. "Who is Mia?"

Daniel gave her a fiery, angry look that she'd never seen before, and his nostrils flared with fury as if she had just struck him physically. "What the hell does she have to do with anything? And who's been talking to you about her?"

A lone tear rolled down Angela's cheek at the realization that Farrah was right. A heaviness filled her belly at the thought that she'd been foolishly wasting her time thinking that Daniel might come to love her as she loved him. He was stuck in the past. "Not you. Why is that, Daniel? Why have you never shared your and Mia's love story?"

Daniel stared back in disbelief at Angela. Who told her? Farrah. Deep down, he'd had a feeling Farrah had told Angela of his history with Mia. It's why she'd been withdrawn after the club. But when she'd responded to him in bed, he'd thought he might be wrong. But he wasn't. Sex was never their problem; communication was.

"I don't want to talk about this," Daniel stated. He walked over to the glass patio doors and stared out at the dark night sky.

"Why not? Who was Mia to you?" Angela pressed, coming up to stand behind him. "It's been over a decade, Daniel. Why can't you talk about her now? Is it because you're still in love with her and you'll never love anyone else?"

Daniel spun around. "Stop it, Angela."

"Why?" she wailed. "I have a right to know. We've been sleeping together for over a month now and if this relationship isn't going anywhere and is a colossal waste of time, then I need to know. I need to know, Daniel."

"Why do you need to know?" He walked as far away from her as he could, to the opposite side of the room. He couldn't think when she was that close, pressing her lush breasts against his back. "This has nothing to do with you. It was another time and place. It doesn't matter now."

"You're fooling yourself, Daniel, because you're not over Mia, and that hurts because you won't share it with me even after everything we've been to each other."

His head began to pound at her anguish. "I don't want to hurt you, Angela." He massaged both of his temples with his hands. "Why are you making this harder than it needs to be? Can't you let this go?"

"I can't because I—" Then she stopped midsentence and her eyes implored him as tears slid down her beautiful cheeks. "Please, I—I just need you to talk to me."

"No!" Daniel walked toward the door and, grabbing his keys off the nearby hook, he opened the door. "I will *not* talk about this."

Seconds later, he was slamming the door shut and heading for the elevator. He knew it was a coward's way out—to walk away from Angela with no explanation—but he couldn't talk about Mia with Angela. It was all jumbled in his head and he needed time to sort through his feelings.

Chapter 20

Angela was so devastated she took the day off. She'd foolishly been banking on one thing: that if she showed Daniel who she truly was, if she was there day in and day out, supporting him, caring for him, loving him, he'd see they shared something real. She wished he could see through her eyes that they had something special to build on. But he couldn't or wouldn't see anything except his past love and hurt.

She didn't know what happened between Daniel and Mia and doubted she ever would. Daniel had closed himself off to her. He'd walked out on her after she'd begged him to let her in. How much more could she put herself on the line and get nothing back in return? How many more times was she going to beat her head against the wall and expect a different result?

It would always be the same.

Daniel was still in love with Mia.

Would always be, just as Farrah had predicted.

Angela had foolishly thought their relationship might be different, but as soon as she'd begun trying to break through the barriers he had around his heart and show him she was there for him and not going anywhere, he'd predictably run scared. A few little items of clothing in his closet had sent him into a panic that she was trying to become a permanent fixture in his life.

And that, Daniel couldn't have.

He wanted to be alone to wallow in his misery of a love gone wrong, or a love unrequited or some other cliché.

She was going to have to move on, but that was going to be difficult given that her professional career was tied to him. She'd only been at Cobb much less than a year. How would it look to a new employer if she bailed so quickly on such an elite firm? They would probably think she couldn't cut the mustard, but she would have to take that risk.

There was no way she could continue to work for Daniel given the state of their relationship. She couldn't bear to watch him date other women and hear the office gossip of the infamous love-'em-and-leave-'em Daniel Cobb. It would crush her spirit if she did.

She needed to figure it out and get her life in order. Facing Daniel would be difficult, but Angela was prepared to do it.

But she didn't have to.

When she returned to work on Wednesday, Daniel didn't show up. She learned from Myrna that he hadn't been there the day before, either. Angela was thankful for the reprieve because it gave her time to put out feelers for a new job. Her old boss had even graciously agreed to allow her to come back if she wanted to. He'd heard how well she was doing at Cobb, but she wasn't keen on that option. The only thing she did know was that she couldn't work at Cobb any longer and would turn in her resignation letter.

She typed it up and had it with her the next morning, prepared to share her decision with Daniel, but he didn't show up. She was worried. Daniel hadn't been absent from the office for three days in the company's existence. She hoped and prayed he was okay.

Everyone in the office was buzzing that no one had heard from him other than a cryptic text he'd sent to Mary to cancel his appointments for the remainder of the week. Despite the heaviness in her chest, Angela knew that she had to leave.

So on Friday, she arrived early before everyone in the office, dressed in jeans and a sleeveless top, and brought boxes with her to pack up her office. She was nearly done when Myrna stopped by her door.

"Do you know what's going on with Daniel?" Myrna inquired.

"Why would I know anything?" Angela asked curtly.

"C'mon, Angela." Myrna closed the office door behind her and came toward her desk. Her blue eyes peered into Angela's. "I know you've been seeing Daniel."

Angela stopped packing up the box. "You're mistaken."

"Well, for starters, Daniel's been MIA for days and you're in here packing. And you don't think I haven't noticed the dark circles under your eyes the last couple of days?" Myrna asked quietly. "Or that you've been crying?"

"Is it that obvious?" Angela reached for her drawer, grabbed her purse and pulled out her compact mirror, searching for any signs. She didn't realize she'd just confirmed Myrna's suspicions until Myrna sat down in front of her.

"Oh, Angela." Myrna shook her head.

Angela glanced up from the mirror. "Please don't say I told you so, because I really can't hear that right now. I know what you said and I didn't listen, okay? So you're right. There. Are you happy now?"

Myrna frowned. "Of course not. I didn't want you to get hurt. Which obviously you are."

"It's my own fault," Angela said, "for wanting more than was on the table."

"Don't blame yourself, Angela. You're a wonderful woman and Daniel is a fool for not realizing that."

"I'm no fool," a masculine voice said from behind them.

Angela glanced up and was startled to find Daniel standing in the doorway of her office. "Daniel!" His name whooshed from her lips.

He was dressed in jeans and a T-shirt. His eyes were bloodshot and there was more than a five o'clock shadow on his jaw. It looked like he hadn't shaved in days. And his eyes were darkened with pain.

"Mr. Cobb." Myrna rose to her feet. "I'm so sorry. I didn't mean—"

He held his hand up, halting her speech. "Myrna, I need a word alone with Angela, please."

She inclined her head. "Of course." She brushed past him quickly, leaving Angela and Daniel alone, staring at each other.

Angela was stunned, not just by Daniel's appearance,

but that he was standing in front of her in pain. He looked like he hadn't slept. He looked as bad as she felt.

"Are you okay?" she asked quietly.

He didn't answer and gave a resigned shrug. He glanced around her office, taking in the upheaval of boxes everywhere. "You're packing?"

Angela didn't answer. Her mouth felt as dry as a bone and she was unable to speak.

"So you're going to leave me, too?"

Too? She was confused. He wasn't making any sense.

Swallowing, Angela found her voice. "What do you want, Daniel?"

"We need to talk."

"You didn't want to talk a few days ago. What's changed now?"

"Please, Angela. I need to talk to you in private. Away from prying eyes." He opened her glass door and held it for her.

Angela noticed that several members of the agency were standing near her office watching the scene unfold between them. He was right. She didn't want to be fodder for office gossip, so she nodded. "All right." She grabbed her purse and walked out past him.

Several sets of eyes followed them as they made their way to the elevator bank. She didn't know what to say as she stood beside Daniel. It was odd to be standing beside him as if they were strangers. But after he'd walked out on her, Angela was at a loss as to what he could possibly want to talk about. Would he tell her how much Mia meant to him?

Quite frankly, she could do without that personal revelation, but he was determined to speak with her so she'd acquiesced.

Once in the garage, she followed him to his car and slid in when he opened the passenger door of his Ferrari. He got in and started the engine.

Angela didn't know where they were going, and Daniel was silent as they drove. When nearly a half hour passed by, she asked, "Where are we going?"

"We'll be there soon."

"That doesn't exactly answer my question," Angela responded, but left it alone.

Eventually, they got off the interstate and after several twists and turns, came to an estate in South Beach. After punching in the code, Daniel drove up the driveway. Shutting off the engine, he came around to open the door, but not before pulling a blanket from his trunk.

Angela stared at the mansion before her. "Daniel, is this one of your clients' homes?"

He nodded. "I've been allowed the use of it for the week while he's out of town."

She snorted. "Must be nice. But if you think you can just romance me into bed with all this—" she motioned toward the luxury home "—then you're mistaken. You can't just shut me up with sex anymore. It won't work."

He stared at her. "I realize that. And that's not why I brought you here. Now will you come with me?" He held out his hand to her while carrying the blanket underneath his other arm.

Angela glanced down at his large masculine hand. She'd come this far, so she would hear him out. She accepted his hand and when she did, a spark of electricity shot through her just as it always did when they touched. They were connected, and Angela forced herself to breathe and not look in his direction.

Instead of going inside, he led her around the side of

the home and keyed in another code, unlocking the side fence. What was on the other side was breathtakingly beautiful. It was a garden oasis far removed from the spice of South Beach, with a luxurious pool and beach house. She would never have known a home like this existed, but then again a lot more doors were open to the wealthy.

She followed Daniel down a pebbled path until eventually they hit the beach. It was secluded and private. She watched Daniel remove his tennis shoes, so she did the same and rolled up her jeans and walked onto the sand.

"I think this is far enough," Angela said. When they made it to the surf, she let go of his hand. "Say what you have to say."

"Walk with me, please."

Angela was torn. If she could, she'd run in the other direction, but another part of her was curious, so she joined him for a walk along the beach.

Daniel was thankful Angela had come with him. He wasn't sure she would agree after he'd left her a few nights ago. He'd had to do a lot of soul-searching and he'd come to realize that he had to let go of the past, and part of that process was sharing it with Angela so he could let her in. Into his life, into his heart.

But it wouldn't be easy. He'd spent years holding on to his hurt like a safety blanket.

Angela walked with him, quietly waiting. It took him several minutes to begin, but eventually he did.

"I met Mia in college," Daniel began. "She was attending Nilson on scholarship. Initially, we were just best friends, living in the same dormitory and helping each other study, but eventually my feelings grew toward her."

Angela stopped short and he could see she was anxious to hear more. "Listen, I get it. No one will ever be Mia or take her place in your heart. Is that why you brought me here, to rub salt in the wound?"

"No, I brought you here so I can tell you some realizations I've come to. But you have to know the entire story. Can you bear with me with, please?"

"I suppose."

"Good."

They walked for a short time until Daniel found a spot between two dunes, out of sight from any beachgoers or onlookers. He placed the blanket on the ground and helped her down before sitting beside her. But they didn't touch.

She sat facing him and he could see wariness and weariness in her eyes. He'd done that to her, and he hated it. He could only hope that what he had to say would make things right between them.

Daniel continued. "By senior year, I thought I was close to winning her over. I foolishly thought that if I bided my time, Mia would see the light and see how well-suited we were for each other. She didn't. Mia didn't want me. She'd had a crush on Ashton Rollins for years. And when he finally paid attention to her, they started seeing each other."

Angela looked at him, confused. She'd probably thought he'd had this great love affair with Mia. How wrong she was.

He laughed. "That's right. She didn't think the great Daniel Cobb was all that. She chose Ashton. He was good-looking and rich and apparently everything she could ever want. And once they began dating, I did my best to be supportive because Mia had no family. Her parents were dead and she'd grown up in the foster care system. She had no one but me. So I stuck around even though it hurt me to watch her with Ashton. But then she was killed in a tragic car accident right after we graduated from college. At her funeral, everyone hovered over her grieving fiancé, Ashton, while the press speculated that Mia might have been drinking, which caused her to lose control of her car. I knew it wasn't true, because Mia didn't drink, but what could I do? And what did it really matter? She was gone. And I was left alone with my regret."

"That if you'd tried harder to win her from Ashton, she'd still be alive?"

He nodded. "I thought that for a long time, but it wouldn't have ever happened. She loved Ashton and not me. It's as simple as that. But Mia's death changed me, Angela. It made me scared. It made me second-guess my judgment when it came to women. And it wasn't just her. When I look back, my parents have never really been a part of my life. There's always been a void there. I closed myself off at a young age and learned not to feel. And I guess after Mia, I never wanted to let anyone get too close for fear of getting hurt again. I tried with Farrah, but she wasn't the right woman. She was only using me to get ahead, and she certainly didn't push me or call me out on my bull crap like you do. *You* were the first person who wasn't willing to back down."

Angela couldn't believe what she was hearing. "And you've come to realize all of this now?"

"Yes. You've opened my eyes and forced me to look at the past and realize that I put Mia on a pedestal as some sort of ideal woman when she was just as human and flawed as both of us. And, most importantly, she was a woman in love with another man. Maybe that's why I was so into her, wanting someone I could never truly have."

"I'm glad that you've come to these realizations," Angela said, turning her hands over and over, "but I'm not sure what this means for you, for me, for us."

"It means I was never really in love with Mia. Just this idealized version of her that I'd carried around in my mind for years. And I know now that it wasn't love. Real love doesn't make you feel bad, or question your self-worth. Real love makes you feel like a king. And I know that because that's how I feel when I'm with you."

"What?" He could see a gamut of perplexing emotions cross her face because he had never spoken of love before, and she probably wasn't sure what it all meant.

So he made it clear.

"I love you, Angela," he confessed. "And I think I've known it for some time, but I've been running scared. Afraid to take a risk again and get hurt. Afraid you might not love me, too. And I'm sorry I made you doubt my feelings for you, but it's true. I love you with all my heart."

"You do?" Hope spread through Angela like wildfire at his admission, but she wasn't jumping in his arms just yet. Was this really happening? Or was she dreaming? Since they'd become involved, Daniel had closed off his heart to her even though she'd given him all of herself. Could she believe what he said was genuine?

She wanted to. It was up to her now to take the risk and tell him how she felt, because he'd just bared his soul to her. Before she could say anything, Daniel spoke again.

"I know you don't need a ring." She watched in shock as he rose to one knee on the blanket. "And I know you aren't looking to be a Mrs." He pulled out a tiny box from his jeans pocket. "But I would very much like to make you one."

Angela's breath caught her in chest. "Oh my God!"

"Angela Trainor, I love you so much and I hope I haven't royally screwed this up, so would you please do me the honor of being my wife? Will you marry me? And before you answer, know that I promise to be committed to you and only you to the day I die."

"Oh, Daniel." Angela threw her arms around him and began kissing him furiously on his neck, cheeks and finally his lips. When she lifted her head, she said, "Do you have any idea how I've longed to hear you say those words?" She cupped his face and in his eyes she saw the love she'd always known was there, but he'd been afraid to let shine. "Because I love you, too. And I have since Key West."

"Since then?"

She nodded. "But I knew you weren't looking for love, for marriage, for any of it. You'd shied away from it for years. You're the media's quintessential bachelor and you played up the role. But I thought if I showed you my love, with my actions, that you'd see it, feel it, know it."

"I knew that night in Key West when we made love that something had shifted between us, that it wasn't just sex anymore. But if I looked too closely I'd have to look inside myself to a place I'd kept hidden until now. I'm just so glad that I haven't lost you, Angela. But you haven't answered my question. Will you marry me?"

"Yes, I will marry you."

Daniel pulled her into his arms and kissed her.

It was the kiss of her dreams.

Hot and demanding, his mouth claimed hers as he took

and tasted all at the same time. His body pressed into hers and Angela welcomed him and the invasion of his tongue in her mouth. She wrapped her fingers around his head and kissed him back. They were possessing each other in a wildly passionate kiss on the blanket in the sand as red-hot desire pulsated between them.

At the contact of his rigid length against her, her nipples hardened and her stomach quivered as heat pooled in her lower half. Daniel hauled her on top of him, clutching her bottom as he molded her against him. She felt his hands on her top, pulling it up and over her head. Then he unfastened her bra and tossed it aside.

Before she knew it, Daniel was rolling her over onto her back, unzipping her jeans and pulling them and her panties off in one swift moment until she was naked. Then he furiously began tearing at his own clothes, eager to be as naked as she was. Neither of them cared where they were, only that they wanted each other and wanted to consummate their love.

It took Daniel only a few seconds to find a condom in his wallet, sheath himself and return to cover Angela's naked body with his. Angela felt a surge of elation when he plunged deep inside her. Wrapping her legs around him, she abandoned herself to the thrust of his hips against hers. She clenched around him, taking him in and enjoying the glorious sensation of having him fill her completely.

He loved her.

He adored her.

It was sheer ecstasy.

She was consumed with happiness so it didn't take long for her to float away as she reached utter satiation.

* * *

"You realize we're both exhibitionists," Daniel said as they lay naked, limbs wrapped around each other and fully satisfied, on the blanket between the dunes.

She smiled. "I guess we are, but there's no place I would rather be."

"I love you, Angela," Daniel said again. Now that he'd said the words aloud, he couldn't stop repeating them. "And I know it's been a whirlwind romance, but I can't wait to make you my wife. The sooner, the better. What do you think of a September wedding? Maybe we could go back to Key West?"

"What's the rush?" Angela laughed, sitting up on one elbow and staring down at him. "If we rush into marriage, people might think we *have* to get married, that you've knocked me up or something."

Daniel's heart began to palpitate and he was a bit breathless when he asked, "You're not pregnant, are you?"

"Of course not," Angela replied. "You do recall how diligent you've been with protection, even just now."

She was right. Despite how overcome with passion he'd been, he had reached for the emergency condom he always kept in his wallet. Of course, he wouldn't need them for too much longer. He couldn't wait for the moment when they were husband and wife and he could dispense with protection. He wanted no barriers between them when they made love.

"Yeah, well, you never know." Daniel shrugged. "Maybe it wouldn't be bad if you were pregnant. I'd like nothing more than to have a little girl with your eyes."

She stared wordlessly across at him. "Neither one of us is ready for a baby any time soon, Daniel. You do realize a glass penthouse is not the ideal place to raise a child."

"Doesn't matter. We can buy a new house. The penthouse has never felt like home anyway. It was just a place I used to shower and sleep until you came along and brightened it with flowers and pictures. You made it home. But you know what that means?"

"What does it mean?"

"We'll just have to find a place that suits the both of us and whatever children may come to be."

"Children, plural?" Angela asked with a raised brow. "How many do you want to have?"

"A few," he answered. Daniel had always hated being the only child and had always wanted brothers and sisters.

"So you're going to keep me barefoot and pregnant?"

"Mmm…" He smiled. "I like the sound of that, but—" he leaned her back onto the blanket "—I have to knock you up first."

He lowered his lips to hers and began making love to her again. Being with Angela felt so good and so right. To be so close to her.

Skin to skin.

Flesh to flesh.

Soft against hard. It was everything he could have ever wanted and more.

Why? Because he'd finally found the woman he was meant to be with. He'd finally found love.

Epilogue

Angela stared at Daniel as he stood next to her parents at their anniversary celebration at the Mezz. She still couldn't believe just how far and how fast their relationship had blossomed. Two months ago, she was just a budding real estate agent working at Daniel's firm. Now she was his fiancée.

She stared down at the three-carat diamond halo ring adorning her third finger. When Daniel had found her packing up her desk, she'd thought that was it. They were over. Finished. Kaput. She couldn't have been more surprised when Daniel finally revealed to her his past infatuation with Mia Landers and how he'd held her up on a pedestal as his ideal woman. A woman who had been in love with Ashton Rollins.

Angela was just thankful that Daniel had come to realize that what they shared was stronger than anything he'd ever felt for Mia. Unlike his college crush, Angela loved him back and would always love him until she was old and gray.

She certainly hoped to share the same kind of marriage her parents did. Even now, thirty years later, they were just as in love as they were when they first wed. Angela could see it as she'd watched them the entire night. She wanted that for her and Daniel.

"They're pretty amazing, huh?" her sister, Denise, asked from her side as she caught Angela eyeing their parents.

Angela glanced in her direction. "I was just thinking how lucky we are that our parents are still together after all these years. And I was just hoping that Daniel and I might one day have the same thing."

Her sister smiled. "You will. I've never seen a man as in love as Daniel is with you. He can't take his eyes off you. Several times tonight, I've caught him staring in your direction when he thought you weren't looking."

"Really?"

"He's besotted with you," Denise said. "And with good reason. You're a great catch."

Angela leaned over and gave her sister a one-armed hug. "Thank you, Denise."

"You're welcome," she replied. "And I have to say, I owe you an apology."

Angela frowned. "For what?"

"This place is great." Denise motioned around the room, which had been decorated with Chiavari chairs, lush linens and large floral centerpieces filled with white roses and crystals and blue uplighting, her parents' favorite color. "You really outdid yourself."

"Thanks." Angela had had a vision, and she'd brought it to life.

"I heard Mom and Dad say how much they love it."

"Love what?" her parents asked, strolling toward them with Daniel. They had caught the tail end of Denise's comment. Daniel came around to Angela's side and slid his arm around her.

"The venue," Denise offered.

"Oh yes, sweetheart," their mother chimed in. "It's exceeded our expectations."

"I'm so glad." Angela beamed with pride. "Only the best for you two."

"Let's toast," Daniel said. He motioned a waiter carrying champagne glasses to bring some over. Once everyone had a flute in their hand, Daniel held up his. "To the happy couple. May you have many more years of wedded bliss."

"To the happy couple."

Daniel was ecstatic to finally hold Angela in his arms. He'd been dying to dance with his fiancée all night, but he'd had business to take care of first. Namely asking Angela's father for her hand in marriage. He knew he'd done it backward and apologized to her father for his haste, admitting he'd been caught up in the moment and pouring out the love he had for his daughter.

Mr. Trainor appreciated his honesty and had given Daniel his blessing. It warmed Daniel's heart because despite her sometimes-strained relationship with her parents, he knew Angela wanted their approval.

And she'd finally gotten it.

"Finally I have you to myself," Daniel said as they swayed to the music.

"We just spent the whole day together."

"Getting ready for the party," he commented. "I meant some quality one-on-one time," he whispered in her ear. Then his tongue flicked out to lightly tease her earlobe.

"Stop that," she murmured.

Instead of stopping, Daniel pulled her even closer, leaned forward and kissed her deeply on the mouth. Her lips were soft on his and it was like a powerful drug to him. He thrust his hips against her in a subtle movement that was meant to arouse, meant to elicit a response.

And it did.

Angela moaned, and her response caused his groin to harden. "What do you say we get out of here?"

"I can't," she said. "Not until they cut the cake."

Daniel groaned. "Spoilsport."

Angela leaned over and in his ear whispered something so naughty and indecent about what she would do to him later that Daniel was relieved no one else could hear. "Promise?" he asked when she raised her head.

"I promise."

Daniel smiled inwardly and wrapped his arm around her waist and then sweetly plundered her mouth. When he finally lifted his head, he said, "I can't wait for tonight, Angela. And for every other night after that I get to spend with you because I love you. I love you so very much."

He kissed the top of her head, and she hugged him back just as tightly. Daniel had found a remarkable woman. A kind, loving, giving woman who would always be by his side. With Angela he'd found his home, his sanctuary.

* * * * *

Puerto Rico is the perfect place to combine business with pleasure. Yet Chloe Chandler can't indulge her attraction to Donovan Rivers when they cross paths at a convention. Heir to an exclusive Long Island venue, Donovan is vying to host the same A-list gala that her parents' restaurant hopes to gain. When the competition comes between them, will their ambitions force them to lose out on love?

Read on for a sneak peek at
IT STARTED IN PARADISE,
the next exciting installment in author Nicki Night's
***THE CHANDLER LEGACY** series!*

Donovan emptied the last of his drink. "You know what's funny?"

"What?" Chloe asked, finally turning to fully face him.

Chloe blinked and Donovan could have sworn time slackened to slow motion. She fixed her doe eyes directly on him.

"We've known each other since we were kids, attended the same schools and lived within the same social circles for years and there's still a lot I don't know about you."

"You're right," Chloe acknowledged.

"We should do something about that." His desire flew past his lips before he had a chance to filter the thought.

Chloe cleared her throat.

"How about dinner tomorrow night?" *Why waste time?* Donovan thought. He wanted to learn more about Chloe Chandler and he had no intentions of toying with his interest. "I know a beautiful place on the other side of the island."

"That should be fine." Chloe looked at her watch and then looked toward the resort's entrance. "Let me check with Jewel and make sure—"

"Just you and me," Donovan interjected.

"Oh…" Chloe's surprise and coyness made him smile once gain.

"I'm sure Jewel wouldn't mind but do check with her to make sure. I wouldn't want her to feel left out." The fact that Jewel had never returned from her "bathroom" run wasn't lost on him. Jewel was rooting for him and he was sure that she was intentionally giving them space.

"I'll do that." Chloe looked at the door again before sitting back.

"It's been a while. I don't think she's coming back," Donovan responded to Chloe's constant looking back toward the hotel.

"Maybe I should go check on her. She did have quite a few of those rum cocktails."

Donovan stood. "Come on." He held his hand out. "I'll walk you to your suite."

Chloe looked at him for a moment before taking his outstretched hand. A quick current shot through him when their palms touched. Donovan liked it. He wondered if she felt it, too, and if she did, had she enjoyed it as much as he had?

Don't miss IT STARTED IN PARADISE
by Nicki Night, available July 2017
wherever Harlequin® Kimani Romance™
books and ebooks are sold.

Get 2 Free Books,

Plus 2 Free Gifts—

just for trying the Reader Service!

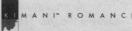

Turn your love of reading into
rewards you'll love with
Harlequin My Rewards

**Join for FREE today at
www.HarlequinMyRewards.com**

Earn **FREE BOOKS** of your choice.

Experience **EXCLUSIVE OFFERS** and contests.

Enjoy **BOOK RECOMMENDATIONS**
selected just for you.

PLUS! Sign up now
and get **500** points
right away!

Earn
FREE
REWARDS
HarlequinMyRewards.com
Join
Today!

MYR16R